LITTI

Little Miss Perfect

Jean Ure

Hodder
Children's
Books

a division of Hodder Headline plc

First published in Great Britain in 2000
by Hodder Children's Books

10 9 8 7 6 5 4 3 2 1

A Catalogue record for this book is available
from the British Library

ISBN 0 340 72726 8

Typeset by Avon Dataset Ltd, Bidford-on-Avon, Warks

Printed and bound in Great Britain by
Clays Ltd, St Ives plc

Hodder Children's Books
a division of Hodder Headline plc
338 Euston Road
London NW1 3BH

1

'Hey, Sam!'

I hammered at Sam's bedroom door and hurled myself through it without bothering to wait for an invitation. This is something I would normally never do. I mean, me and Sam are really strict about our privacy, but I was bursting. Did I have news for her!

'What is it?' said Sam. Not sounding too pleased, I must admit. Well, I wouldn't have, either. It's very bad manners to go crashing into people's bedrooms like that. But this was important! This was something that affected both of us.

'We're having another!' I wailed.

'Holy hog wash!'

Me and Sam had just got in from school. Sam had gone straight upstairs to change out of her school uniform – Sam really hates school uniform – while I'd stayed in the hall to say hallo to Jack, who's my dog. (Daisy is Sam's. She'd gone galloping upstairs with Sam.)

While me and Jack were rolling about the floor, having a bit of a smooch and a cuddle, I heard Mum's voice on the telephone. I wasn't eavesdropping; it just came drifting out into the hall.

I heard her say, 'Yes, of course! I'm sure we could manage. Just for a few weeks . . . no problem! Bring her along. We'll cope, we always do.'

I knew at once what it meant. It meant that Miss Davies from Social Services had rung to ask if we could take another foster child.

'She said, after Bella—' Sam danced about, hauling up her jeans. She likes to wear them really tight, which means she sometimes has difficulty getting into them. 'She said she was going to give it a rest for a bit!'

'I know that's what she *said*.'

Me and Sam hadn't got on too well with Bella. (Not until after she'd left, when we'd suddenly

2

felt kind of fond of her.) Mum had promised that, as we were starting at our new school that term, and would have enough to cope with, she wouldn't take any more fosters for a while.

'Give you a chance to settle in,' she'd said.

We'd been somewhat relieved, as it is quite stressful having a new person in the house, having to be polite all the time and consider their feelings and to *make allowances*. Mum is always telling us that we have to make allowances. We try! We do try. But with some people it is not easy.

It is almost never easy, just at first. When our little brother Gus (known as the Radish because of his red hair) came to us, he was so timid he just clung to Mum's legs and wouldn't say a word. We thought he'd never learn to trust us. But he did in the end and now we love him to bits. We're even hoping to adopt him!

Sam never had those kind of problems because Sam is – well! Sam is Sam and what Mum calls 'a law unto herself'. She just bounced in and took over! Her and me have been best friends from the very beginning. We're like sisters.

All the other people we foster, they just come and go. Sometimes they're with us for a month or two, sometimes just for a few weeks. Mum is such a softie! She can never say so.

I do understand how she feels. If it was animals, I would be just the same. I would have a houseful!

But animals are easier to get on with than human beings.

'I just hope it's not another Bella,' grumbled Sam.

Bella had been *so* boastful. But even Bella hadn't been all bad. We'd had some fun with her.

'Let's go down and find out,' I said.

Sam pulled on her T-shirt and we went racing downstairs, with Jack and Daisy at our heels, to confront Mum.

She was in the kitchen with the Radish. The Radish was laying the table and Mum was making some tea. She didn't *look* like a person with a guilty secret, but she did give this little start as we came stampeding through the door.

'Oh! Sam and Abi,' she said. 'Just in time.'

Maybe she only started 'cos we took her by surprise. But somehow I didn't think so!

I cried, 'Mum, is it true? Are we really going to have another one?'

Her cheeks went bright scarlet.

'Another what?' she said. As if she didn't know!

'Another foster,' said Sam.

'Oh – well. Yes!' Mum gave a little laugh. Definitely guilty!

'*Anudder* one?' said the Radish.

Even he was staring at Mum accusingly.

'You said you were going to give us time to settle in.' I stared at her accusingly, as well.

'Abi!' said Mum. 'You have settled in! You told me only the other day how much you were enjoying it.'

'I didn't say *enjoying* it,' I muttered.

It was true that moving up to secondary school

had been no big deal. Practically everybody from our year had moved with us, so it wasn't like we were with strangers. All the same, I did think Mum should have stood firm just this once.

'It's only three weeks since Bella went!'

'Yes, I know,' said Mum.

'You're too *easy*,' I said. I said it very sternly. Mum hung her head.

'Yes,' she said. 'I know.'

'Miss Davies just twists you right round her little finger. *Oh, Mrs Foster, I wonder could you help us out? We've got this dear little baby—*'

'*Just one week old.*' That was Sam, joining in.

'*Its mummy doesn't want it—*'

'*Poor little thing!*'

'*If you don't take it, Mrs Foster, I don't know what we'll do.*'

'*We'll have to flush it down the toilet!*'

'Ugh! Sam,' I said. 'Don't be disgusting!'

Mum was laughing, but she did look a bit shamefaced.

'It's very difficult,' she pleaded. 'How can you say no when there's a child in need?'

Sam looked at me and rolled her eyes.

'You're such a sucker!' she told Mum.

'I know, I know! But it's only till the end of term.'

'The end of *term*?' That was months away! We'd only been back a fortnight. 'What's Dad going to say?'

'Oh, he'll say what he always says!' Mum cheered up immediately at the mention of Dad. She knew he'd always back her, no matter what. '*You do your own thing. I'm easy.*'

Dad *is* easy. He says you have to be, in his line of business. He's a plumber. He says when you're dealing with people and pipes, you have to be philosophical. Meaning, just go with the flow. (Ha ha! That's a plumbing joke.) Dad probably wouldn't mind if Mum gave house room to a dozen foster children.

'So what is it,' said Sam, 'anyway?'

'You mean, *who* is it,' said Mum. 'It's a little

girl called Anna. Anna Margolis. She sounds really sweet.'

Sweet! I could almost hear Sam going *yuck*. Sweet is a real turn-off, you must admit.

'How little?' I said.

I was hoping Mum would say two, or three, or even four. A toddler wouldn't be so bad. I mean, for one thing we wouldn't be expected to cart it round with us. But to Mum, anyone under the age of about twenty is little. So I wasn't really surprised when she said that sweet little Anna was ten.

Me and Sam exchanged glances. Ten was a *bad* age. Almost the worst. Old enough for Mum to think we should do things with her, but still a whole year younger than me and Sam and bound to be incredibly babyish. Compared with eleven-year-olds, I mean.

I sighed, and Sam scowled.

'Why's it coming to us?'

'Sam! Don't keep saying *it*,' said Mum. 'She's coming because she's got nowhere else to go.

She lost her mum a year or so back and she's been living with her nan, but her nan's just died and her dad's working abroad and can't get home till the end of term, so she needs someone to look after her until then. She won't be any trouble! You'll hardly notice she's here.'

'Why?' said Sam. 'Is she going to live in a cupboard?'

The Radish squealed and pummelled his cheeks. He thought that was really funny! Mum flapped at Sam with a tea towel.

'Stop it! How would you have felt if we'd said things like that about you before you came?'

'Prob'ly did,' said Sam.

'We didn't,' I assured her. 'We were looking forward to it.'

'Yes, we were,' said Mum. 'And to Gus.' She gave him a cuddle. (The Radish needs a lot of cuddling.) 'So why are you making all this fuss about poor little Anna? Abi, why are *you* making such a fuss? You were the one who wanted us to foster!'

'I still do,' I said. 'But Bella was such a pain!' All up front and in your face. I didn't think I could take another one like her!

'Bella had a lot to put up with,' said Mum. 'She had a lot of unhappiness in her life. So has Anna, poor little soul! But you'll find her quite different from Bella. She's a quiet little thing, according to Miss Davies. Very self-contained. She won't interfere in your precious business.'

'Hmm!' snorted Sam.

Sam didn't sound very convinced. I wasn't sure that I was, either. Bella had wanted to be in on absolutely everything. If we went into the garden, she'd come cramming out with us. If we shut ourselves in our bedrooms, she came banging at the door.

'Where's it go to school?' said Sam, plonking herself down at the table and snatching at a piece of bread and jam.

'Would you mind rephrasing that?' said Mum.

'Which school's it go to?' said Sam.

Sam can be really stroppy at times!

'I shall not answer that,' said Mum. 'I don't know anyone called "It".'

'Anna,' said the Radish. He explained it to Mum, very earnestly. 'She meanth *Anna*.'

'Yes, I thought she did,' said Mum. 'But until she asks the question properly—'

'*Anna!*' roared Sam, spitting bread and jam across the table. 'Where is *Ann*-ah going to school?'

I thought Mum would tell her off for being rude, but sometimes Mum lets Sam get away with things that she wouldn't dream of letting me get away with. It's because of Sam being a foster, and allowances having to be made. Like every time a new foster child comes into the house, especially if it's a girl and the same age as us, Mum worries in case Sam gets to feeling insecure and thinking Mum and Dad might prefer the new one and decide to send Sam back to the children's home. They wouldn't, of course. Sam's part of the family! But Mum says when you've spent the first years of your life being pushed around from pillar to post,

11

you find it difficult to believe that at last you're loved and wanted.

So she didn't tell Sam not to shout, or not to talk with her mouth full. She simply said, 'Anna goes to school in Southover Park.'

'But that's nowhere near!' I sat down opposite Sam. 'How's she going to get there?'

'We'll work something out. I might have to take her in by car.'

'Then you'll be one of the school-run mums who pollute the atmosphere and clutter the roads up,' said Sam.

'Well! It can't be helped. She's a bit too young to make the journey by herself.'

'Destroying the ozone layer,' muttered Sam.

'It's only till the end of term. Don't be so self-righteous!'

'We've already got global warming.' Sam crammed another piece of bread and jam into her mouth. 'Before we know it, there'll be sharks swimming in the Thames. That's official,' she added. 'I read it in the paper.'

'And I suppose it will be all my fault,' said Mum.

'Why can't she go to school locally?' I said.

'Because she's had quite enough upset in her life without having to change schools. In any case, she goes to ballet school in Southover and she certainly can't change ballet schools. She has five lessons a week,' said Mum. 'She's hoping to do it professionally.'

'What, ballet dancing?' Sam pulled one of her faces.

'Now what's your problem?' said Mum.

'*Bally* dancing. That is really naff,' said Sam.

'What do you mean, it's naff? Don't be so silly!'

'It is,' said Sam. 'It's for dweebs and dorks. It's naff!'

Sam is full of these weird prejudices. I try not to be, though sometimes I find you can't help it. Like, I have this simply huge prejudice against people who don't like animals. Anyone who doesn't like animals, I don't like them! But I didn't have anything against ballet. Not specially. I mean, I'd seen some on television once, and it seemed OK.

'It's girly,' said Sam.

'So what's wrong with girly?' Mum wanted to know.

'All pink and pretty. *Ugh!*'

Sam made one of her being-sick noises. The Radish promptly copied her.

'Men do ballet,' said Mum.

Blurgh, went Sam. *Blurgh*, went the Radish.

'And it isn't all pink and pretty! Some of it's very athletic.'

Blurgh, went Sam.

Blurgh, went the Radish.

'Oh, I give up!' said Mum.

'This is ballet.'

Sam sprang up from the table and began prancing round the kitchen, waving her arms with her fingers pointed, a simpering smile on her lips.

'Thith ith ballet!'

The Radish began doing it, too. He just loves to copy.

'Knees bend ... oops!' went Sam, banging her bum against the kitchen cabinet.

'Kneeth bend ... ooopth!' went the Radish, sticking his bottom in the air.

'Now I'm being a fairy ... look at me! Being a fairy!'

'Fairy!' echoed the Radish.

They both jumped on to chairs and stood there with their arms above their heads and one leg stretched out behind them, only the Radish couldn't keep his balance and fell over and bumped his head, which immediately set him off howling.

'Now see what you've done,' scolded Mum. She hauled the Radish on to her lap. 'That'll teach you to make fun!'

'Won't teach me!' boasted Sam, leaping to the ground and cavorting round the kitchen. 'I don't need teaching! I can do it all by myself!'

'Is this girl – I mean, Anna,' I said, 'is she really going to be a dancer?'

'Oh, yes,' said Mum. 'She's serious. Not just playing at it. She's hoping to go to ballet school full-time next year. She's really dedicated.'

I was impressed! I think it's really cool to be dedicated. I would like to be dedicated myself. I am exceedingly interested, for example, in colours and materials and in fact anything to do with the world of art. Before we started at secondary school I used to have special art classes on a Saturday morning. I only gave them up because Mum was worried it might interfere with the vast amounts of homework we now had to do. But although I would very much like to go to art college when I leave school I couldn't honestly say that I am *dedicated* to it, in the way that people are dedicated to being, for instance, ice skaters or tennis players or ballet dancers.

I looked at Sam, still hopping and skipping about the kitchen, waving her legs in the air and pulling silly faces, and I thought that perhaps this Anna person might turn out to be quite interesting. Even if she was only ten years old!

2

'I knew someone who was a ballet dancer.'

It was next day, at school. We were standing in the playground during mid-morning break with a group of other people from our class. There was Mary-Jo Mitchell and her best friend Lissie Thomas; Susha Patel and Kayleigh Morgan; and a girl called Jasmine Potter who wasn't really one of us but just hung about.

'It was this girl that lived next door to my nan. She was dead boring,' said Mary-Jo. 'She used to practise all this ballet stuff all the time, and she couldn't ever play rounders or hockey or anything in case she got injured. She couldn't even go horse riding,' she added, for Lissie's benefit. Lissie is mad about horses!

'Why couldn't she go horse riding?' said Lissie.

'I dunno.' Mary-Jo scrunched up her face,

trying to remember. 'She told me, once, but I couldn't understand it . . . something about developing the wrong muscles.'

Sam made a loud scoffing noise. It sounded like 'Pah!'

'Well, but you would,' said Jasmine.

Everyone turned to look at her. What did she know about it?

'You would,' she insisted. 'All that *squeezing*.'

'What squeezing?' said Sam.

'With your knees! To get the horse going. It'd make your thigh muscles bulge.'

'My thigh muscles don't bulge,' said Lissie. And she held up her skirt to show us. 'Do my thigh muscles bulge?'

'N-no,' said Mary-Jo. 'Not *bulge*, exactly. But this girl that I knew, the one I was telling you about, her legs were thin as thin. I mean, even her thighs. Like you know when you sit on something and they all kind of flob out? Like this!'

Mary-Jo perched herself on top of a nearby rail

and we all stood watching as her thighs flattened and flobbed.

'I mean, that's *normal*,' she told us, earnestly. 'It's what thighs ought to do. But this girl's didn't. They looked like garden canes! She couldn't ever eat properly, in case she put on weight. All she used to eat was low-fat yoghurt and carrots and stuff.'

That alarmed me, I have to admit. I didn't like the sound of that one little bit! Mum had already hinted, when Bella was with us, that me and Sam ought to eat less junk food. I didn't want to be put on a diet of carrots and low-fat yoghurt, thank you very much!'

'*Dead* boring,' said Mary-Jo.

'Dead *stupid*, if you ask me,' said Sam.

'Yes, but it's what you have to do if you're a dancer. You have to be thin or you can't dance.'

'Who'd want to?' jeered Sam.

'This girl did. She wanted to dance in ballet more than anything else in the world.'

'Must have been mad!'

There was a silence, while we pondered it.

'I saw a ballet once,' said Kayleigh. 'It was kind of—'

'What?' I said.

'Well . . . kind of pretty,' said Kayleigh.

'Pretty?' Sam made another of her scoffing noises. 'It's poncy! Poncy and girly and *naff*!'

And she set off in a circle doing this swaying kind of dance, rippling her arms and flapping her eyes and teetering about on her tippity toes. Mary-Jo at once joined in, and then so did Lissie, and Jasmine and all the rest of us, even me, we were all at it, rippling and flapping and smiling these sweet sickly smiles. This was ballet! Poncy and girly and naff.

I didn't really think it was like that. What I'd seen on television had been quite funny, actually. There'd been a man dressed up as a woman, doing a clog dance. He kept falling out of his clogs and tripping over his own feet, and I'd squealed with laughter. Of course, I'd been younger then. A whole lot younger. Maybe now

I'd find it a bit childish. But I was still curious! I still wondered what Anna would be like. What she would look like, how she would behave. I'd never met a truly *dedicated* person before. They had to be different from the rest of us!

On the way home at the end of school Sam said, 'See? I told you! It's going to be a food nutter and starve itself. Then Mum'll start on at us again about not eating crisps and then you'll be sorry!'

'I didn't invite it here!' I said.

'No, but you're all eager,' said Sam. 'Secretly you're looking forward to it!'

'I'm not looking forward to it!'

'Yes, you are!'

'Look,' I said, 'I am *not*. And don't keep calling her it! You know it gets Mum mad.'

I'd thought Anna might already be there when we got in, but Mum said Miss Davies was collecting her after her dancing class and bringing her over.

'At least it means we can eat our *tea*,' said

21

Sam, making a grab for a chocolate roll. 'After tomorrow—' she put her face close to mine and hissed it at me: 'Raw carrots!'

'Do you mind?' I said. 'I can see all inside your mouth!'

'What's this about raw carrots?' Mum wanted to know.

'Nothing,' I said hastily. I didn't want to go putting ideas into Mum's head. But Sam couldn't resist.

'It's what *bally* dancers eat . . . raw carrots and yoghurt.'

Mum immediately looked flustered.

'Miss Davies didn't say anything about a special diet! I should have thought about that. I'll have to ask her.'

'Oh, Mum, don't!' I begged.

I saw this really bleak future with the cupboard full of muesli bars and dried apricots (ugh! I can't stand dried apricots). Not a bag of crisps or a chocolate bar in sight. Life wouldn't be worth living!

'Well, it's possible she has to watch her weight,' said Mum. And then she added, 'Ridiculous, at her age! Though I'm all for healthy living. *Sam!*' She slapped at Sam's hand as it reached out for its third chocolate roll. 'Two each! You've had your two.'

'See?' said Sam. 'It's started!'

After tea, me and Sam took the dogs up to the park for their walk. We'd just got back and were cleaning their feet in the kitchen ('cos the park was really muddy) when there was a knock at the front door.

'That'll be her!'

The dogs ran barking into the hall before we could stop them. Mum shot out of the front room crying, 'Sam, Abi, get those dogs—'

'*Under control!*' chorused me and Sam.

It's what Mum always says when we have a new foster coming.

'Well, go on, then,' she said, 'do it! Get them back in the kitchen and keep them there.'

Sam picked up Daisy, I picked up Jack, and we

hotfooted it down the hall. There's always this worry, just at first, in case the new foster is scared of dogs. Like with the Radish. I'd had to shut poor Jack in my bedroom for the first few days when the Radish came to us. Sam, of course, wasn't fazed. Sam isn't fazed by anything. She'd just giggled when Jack jumped up. But a dancer . . .

'Bet she screams her head off,' said Sam.

Anna didn't scream her head off. The dogs had calmed down a bit by the time Mum finally brought her out into the kitchen. Daisy rushed over to say hallo, and Jack barked and bounced, and Anna simply – took no notice of them! It was really weird. How can you *not* take notice of two eager dogs?

Mum said afterwards that she had told Anna just to ignore them and they would settle down, and that is exactly what she did! Just brushed past them and sat herself down at the table without even a pat or a word of greeting.

I couldn't do that, myself. If an animal says

hallo to me I think it is only civil to say hallo back. After all, they have their feelings just as we do.

'Anna, this is Abi. This is Sam,' said Mum. 'We've just had tea and we'll be eating again when Dad gets in, about six o'clock. Would you like a sandwich or something to keep you going?'

'That would be lovely,' said Anna.

'What would you like in it? Cheese? Chocolate spread? Peanut butter? Or how about lettuce and Marmite?'

Well! She chose the lettuce and Marmite. It seemed like a bad sign. Sam dug me rather hard in the ribs and I dug her back.

'Why don't you two girls sit down and keep Anna company?' said Mum.

I didn't get the feeling that Anna particularly wanted company. She seemed sort of – I don't know how to put it – like she had this plastic bubble round her. Not shy. Just . . . enclosed in her own little world. Like other people didn't really exist.

But we obediently sat down and watched as she ate her boring old lettuce and Marmite sandwich. She ate amazingly fast! I'd have thought, being a dancer, she'd have picked at things. Just nibbled round the edges, all fastidious and dainty.

She *looked* fastidious and dainty. She was about my height, even though she was a year younger (I am not very tall, alas) but loads skinnier. She had long black hair, pulled back into a pony tail, and this very delicate face with big dark eyes and a tiny little nose. Not tiny the way mine is tiny. Mine is – well! I think I have to be honest. My nose is *snub*. Like a button that's been stuck on as an afterthought. Anna's was short and neat and sort of . . . modelled. Like someone had gone to a lot of trouble carving it out of ivory. (Only not ivory 'cos that is elephants' tusks and is got by cruel means.)

My first thought when I looked at her was that her head was like a beautiful flower on a graceful stem. Sam would say that sounded *dead yucky*, and I would have to agree with her. But it is what I thought.

'We have a bit of a problem,' said Mum, suddenly.

Sam's head shot round. So did mine. Now what?

'Anna needs somewhere to practise. There's not enough space in the spare bedroom. So I was wondering . . . would either of you two girls be willing to change rooms? Just until the end of term?'

I was sitting next to Sam, and I could feel her stiffen.

'I know it's a lot to ask,' said Mum, 'but—'

But what? Me and Sam regarded Mum, with these stony expressions on our faces. The spare room is tiny! It's like a broom cupboard. How could Mum expect either of us to exist in a broom cupboard for the next three months?

'I could ask Gus,' she said (meaning: The *Radish* wouldn't mind). 'But his room's hardly any bigger.'

Sam and me had the biggest rooms in the house. Bedrooms, that is. And mine is the biggest of all, 'cos I got to have first choice before Sam came here.

On the other hand, Sam doesn't have as much stuff as I do. I have all my books and my ornaments and my desk and my easel and my dolls' house that I practise my interior decorating on. Practising my interior decorating was just as important as Anna practising her ballet!

On the other hand again, Sam likes to have space for practising her gym. She does handstands against the wall, and stretches her body into weird shapes, and rolls about on the floor. It was just as important for Sam to practise her gym as for me to practise my interior decorating.

It was important for both of us, and it wasn't fair of Mum to ask.

There was a long silence. Anna just went on eating her sandwich. The dogs sat one on either side of her; looking at her so sweetly! She still didn't take any notice of them.

'Well?' said Mum. She said it all brightly. 'Any offers?'

Sam tilted her chair back, with her knees balanced against the table. I heaved a sigh.

'Abi?' Mum was on to it immediately.

'I s'ppose I could,' I mumbled. 'But I don't know where all my stuff's going to go!'

Mum gave me this big happy beam.

'We could put some of it in Sam's room, maybe. Or in Gus's.'

'Mm. I s'ppose.'

'It's only for a short time,' pleaded Mum. 'I'll make it up to you, I promise! We're very grateful, aren't we, Anna?'

'Yes.' Anna nodded, and her pony tail lifted and fell.

'Come on, then!' said Mum. 'Let's go and do it while we're waiting for your dad.'

Sam went off to watch telly with the Radish, but I went upstairs with Mum and Anna. If my room was going to be taken apart, I wanted to be there to supervise!

We put the books in the Radish's room and the desk and the dolls' house in Sam's. I took the ornaments and the easel. I really hated being without my dolls' house – I've had it since I was six years old. My dad made it for me – but I couldn't live without the easel. I was into painting, now. In a big way!

'I'm really worried about the light,' I said to Mum. 'There's not enough light in this titchy little room!'

'We'll get you an Anglepoise,' said Mum.

Mum doesn't understand about painting! You can't paint by *Anglepoise*. You need proper light. I thought maybe what I'd do, if the weather was good, I'd take my paints downstairs and paint in the garden.

The bedroom looked really bare with all my stuff taken out of it.

'Right,' said Mum. 'Let's get your things in here, Anna.'

The bedroom still looked bare! All she'd

brought with her were her clothes, a few books (ballet ones), some pictures (all of ballet dancers), and a suitcase full of ballet gear. Hair bands, leotards, things that I thought were bedsocks but which turned out to be leg warmers, tights – dozens of them! – and ballet shoes. Mostly pink.

I was disappointed in the ballet shoes. I'd thought they'd be shiny satin but they were just ordinary leather and some of them were really scuffed and tatty.

'What about the hard bits at the end for when you stand on your toes?' I said. 'Where are the hard bits?'

'There aren't any hard bits,' said Anna. 'It's called going on point and I haven't gone on to my points yet.'

I wondered why not. I started to ask her, but Mum came into the room carrying what looked like a miniature clothes rack and said, 'Where would you like this, Anna?'

'What is it?' I said.

'It's a portable barre.' Anna took it from Mum

and set it up in the middle of the room where there was most space.

'What's it for?'

'It's for barre work.'

I didn't like to ask her what barre work was – I mean, there's a limit to the amount of ignorance you can display – but I think she could see I was dying to know 'cos she said, 'Would you like me to show you?'

'Yes, show Abi what you do,' said Mum, 'while I go down and see to the supper.'

Honestly, Mum is so transparent at times! I could almost hear her thinking, 'Oh, this is good! Abi is taking an interest. I can leave them to get to know each other.'

'This is barre work,' said Anna.

She placed a hand on the clothes rail.

'We'll start with *pliés*.' I watched as she did what seemed to be an ordinary knees bend, except more graceful.

'These are positions of the feet . . . first position.' She turned her feet out so that they were in a straight line, heel to heel. I'd never seen feet go like that before! 'Second position . . . third position—'

There were five in all. But the one that really impressed me was the first! Feet in a straight line! I wanted to rush away and try it out for myself. (I didn't like to try it in front of Anna in case I couldn't do it, which would make me look stupid.)

'These are *battements tendus*—'

Battermon tondew? I looked puzzled. What was she talking about?

'It's French,' said Anna. 'Ballet's always in French.'

She started sliding one leg out to the side, pointing her foot, then sliding her leg back in again. It was kind of fascinating.

'*Ronds de jambe à terre* . . . *battements frappes* . . . *arabesque.*'

She left the clothes rail and standing on one leg stretched the other really high behind her. It was way up in the air, over her head! I felt almost certain I'd never be able to get mine that high, and even if I did I'd probably fall over. Anna didn't even wobble.

'It's a bit like gym,' I said, 'isn't it?'

'Well . . . sort of,' said Anna.

Sam's good at gym. I am *not*. But I still couldn't resist sneaking out into the garden while Mum was getting the supper and Sam (I *thought*) was still watching the telly and having a go at some of the things I'd seen Anna do.

I used a branch of the apple tree as a barre. It was a bit too high, really, but it was something to hold on to. First I tried making my feet go in a straight line, heel to heel, the way Anna had done. They wouldn't go! The most I could get them into was a sort of fan shape. Even then my ankles kept rolling all over the place.

So I gave up on that and tried the knees bends, instead. The *pliés*. Even they weren't as easy as Anna had made them look. When she did them, her heels stayed on the ground till the very last minute: mine came up almost immediately! It was very frustrating.

Embarrassing, too! 'Cos I suddenly heard Sam's dulcet tones. (This is what our music teacher at school says. 'Dulcet tones', when someone's singing all raucous and out of tune and he wants to be sarcastic.)

'Abi! What on earth are you doing?'

'Nothing,' I said, quickly. (Turning as red as a pillar box.)

'I caught you!' crowed Sam. 'I caught you doing poncy ballet!'

'It's not poncy.'

'Yes, it is! It's poncy! *I* wouldn't have given my bedroom up.'

'No, I noticed,' I said.

'Well, why should I? Why should either of us? It's not fair!'

It wasn't fair. But no one had made me: I had offered. I wondered why I'd done it.

'It's only till the end of term,' I muttered.

'That's ages away. You must be mad!'

Sam grabbed hold of the apple tree branch

and began dipping and bending, throwing her legs up, first in front, then behind.

'See?' she said. 'It's easy! Anyone can do it!'

What was annoying was that Sam was doing it almost as well as Anna. Just not quite as gracefully.

'Bet you can't do first position!' I said.

'What's first position?'

'Turning your feet out sideways. Like this.' I turned my feet out as far as they would go. 'Except they're supposed to be in a straight line.'

'Like this?'

It was *so* annoying! Sam's feet turned out far further than mine did.

'It's still not a straight line,' I said.

'Straighter than yours!'

'When Anna does it, it's *dead* straight.'

'It's unnatural, anyway,' declared Sam. 'Feet aren't meant to be turned out sideways. Not unless you're a duck!'

And she went waddling off up the garden with her feet splayed out, going 'Quack, quack, quack!'

I decided that I would practise in secret, in my horrid little bedroom, until my feet, too, were in a dead straight line. If Anna could do it, I didn't see any reason I couldn't!

3

'Veggie burgers and chips,' said Mum. She looked at Anna, all anxiously. 'Are you sure that's all right for you, Anna? Or would you rather I did you a salad?'

It was Monday evening. Dad had just got in and we were sitting round the kitchen table. Anna had been with us for four days, but Mum still hadn't got used to the idea that she could feed her just the same as she fed the rest of us. We needn't have worried about raw carrots and yoghurt! Anna didn't seem to be at all fussed about her weight. I mean, to be fair, she didn't pig out on snacks between meals, but whatever Mum put on her plate, she gobbled it up. She ate *really* fast. It was strange, for such a tiny, dainty-looking person. But it was a real relief to me and Sam, I can tell you!

'I can do you a salad if you'd rather.' Mum

was still hovering, holding the chips high in the air as if they might suddenly descend upon Anna with a great fatty *glug*! and make her swell up like a balloon. 'It won't take a second.'

'No, really,' said Anna. 'It's quite all right.'

'Well, if you're sure,' said Mum.

'Honestly,' said Anna.

She was always *incredibly* polite.

'It wouldn't be any trouble,' said Mum, plonking the chips on the table and running across to the refrigerator. 'It's all here, I'd only have to wash it.'

I could feel Sam squirming, next to me. I felt a bit squirmy myself. Mum had never gone to all this bother over any other of our fosters!

'There's lettuce, tomato, radishes, cucumber . . . do you like cucumber?'

'*Mum!*' I said.

'What?'

'She doesn't *want* salad!'

'I think what she's trying to tell you,' said Dad, 'is that she's perfectly happy with burger

39

and chips. Isn't that right, Anna?'

He winked at her, but all she said, big-eyed, was, 'Truly, I don't mind.'

She didn't have very much sense of humour; I'd already noticed that. I mean, if Dad had winked at me and Sam, or even the Radish, we'd have giggled and agreed with him. We'd have liked the idea of being in league against Mum!

'Well, so long as I'm not going to get into trouble for feeding you the wrong food,' said Mum. 'I know you young dancers have to watch your weight.'

Mum, I thought. Don't go pushing people into anorexia!

Sam actually said it out loud. (She's bolder than me.)

'Mum, you shouldn't go pushing people into anorexia!'

'Oh. Well, no,' agreed Mum, getting flustered. 'Of course not! I didn't mean—' she waved a hand. 'I didn't mean don't *eat*. I meant—'

She meant it was OK for the rest of us to have

burger and chips 'cos we were just ordinary mortals. Anna was a dancer. She was *special*.

'Why don't you sit down and get on with your food and stop blethering?' said Dad. He didn't say it unkindly. But Mum was getting so fussed! 'I'm sure Anna's quite capable of deciding for herself.'

Anna speared a couple of chips on the end of her fork.

'Miss Heriot says that while you're young you need to build your strength up.'

Miss Heriot was Anna's dancing teacher. She'd once been a dancer herself, with the Royal Ballet Company. Anna had a photo of her on her bedroom wall. My bedroom wall.

'Miss Heriot is absolutely right,' said Dad. 'Especially if you're doing something as energetic as ballet . . . using up all those calories! I should think you burn everything off the minute you've eaten it.'

Anna nodded. 'That's what my nan used to say.'

We all fell silent at the mention of her nan. It was only two weeks since she had died and Anna had lived with her since she was eight years old. Surely she must still be upset?

'You must miss your nan very much,' said Mum, gently.

'Yes.' Anna speared another chip. 'I do, but she was quite old.'

I don't think even Mum knew what to say to that. Did being quite old mean that you didn't matter so much?

'How old was she?' said Sam.

I told you Sam was bold! I wouldn't have dared to ask that question.

'She was almost eighty,' said Anna.

'One of my nans is almost eighty,' I said. 'Isn't she?' I looked at Dad. 'Big Nana's almost eighty?'

'She is that,' agreed Dad.

I noticed that Mum was frowning at me and shaking her head. She said afterwards, 'Anna was very fond of her nan. We have to be careful how we talk about it.'

'Well, but she was the one who mentioned her!' I said.

'Yes, I know,' said Mum. 'On the surface she appears to have taken it very well. But underneath she must still be upset.'

I supposed that Mum was right; she usually is. I'd certainly be upset if one of my nans had died.

As soon as we'd finished eating our first course, Anna asked if she could leave the table.

'You don't want any pudding?' said Mum. 'It's not stodge! It's only ice cream.'

But Anna was sure she wanted to go upstairs and do some practice.

'Again?' said Mum. 'I thought you did some earlier?'

'Only a little bit. I need to do more.' Anna looked at Mum solemnly out of her big dark eyes. 'I always do on days I don't have class.'

'Well, all right,' said Mum, 'but don't overdo it.'

'I won't,' promised Anna. 'I know when to stop.'

The door closed behind her, but we didn't actually hear her going up the stairs. She was ever so quiet. If it had been me or Sam you'd have heard us all right! Sam always goes upstairs in great leaps and bounds. I tend to flump. And the stairs go creak and moan.

They didn't creak and moan when Anna went up them. It was like her feet hardly touched the floor.

'I suppose she knows what she's doing,' said Mum. 'All this practice . . . she never seems to do anything else!'

'She's dedicated,' I said.

'I hope she's not doing it because of being upset over her nan.'

'Mum! She's *dedicated*. It's what people do when they're dedicated.'

'How would you know?' said Sam.

'It's like that girl Mary-Jo was telling us about.'

'The one that only ate carrots!'

I kicked at Sam under the table. 'The one that practised all the time. And *don't start on about the carrots*,' I hissed, as Mum clattered dirty dishes on to the draining board.

Sam shrugged.

'She's certainly a very together little thing,' said Dad. 'Very focused. Knows exactly where she's going.'

'Yes. An old head on young shoulders,' said Mum.

'She could teach that pair a thing or two,' said Dad.

He said it in a jokey kind of way, but still looking rather hard at me and Sam. We were in bad odour with Dad just at the moment. That was how Mum had put it: *bad odour*. Meaning, I suppose, that we were like a particularly nasty kind of smell. We'd been messing around in the garden, playing with Jack and Daisy, and Sam had crashed into Dad's new cucumber frame with me on top of her. Fortunately he hadn't yet got around to putting any glass in it, so we didn't hurt ourselves. Just busted up his frame.

It wasn't the sort of thing that Anna would ever do.

'She's amazingly mature,' agreed Mum.

Sam looked at me and we scrunched our faces into gargoyle expressions.

'*Boring!*' said Sam.

After tea the Radish wanted us to play with him but I said that I had things to do.

'What things?' said Sam.

'Her homework, I should hope,' said Mum.

'We haven't got any homework! Miss Mailer was away and didn't set any.'

'I've still got things to do,' I said.

I'd sort of toyed with the idea of taking my easel down to the garden and doing some painting, just to show that I was every bit as dedicated (in my own way) as Anna. But the light wasn't really good enough and I wasn't feeling all that inspired, so instead I went and knocked on Anna's door. My door.

I didn't go bursting in because that is always bad manners, specially with a guest. But I did hope she'd open the door quickly before Sam came galloping upstairs!

'Abi.' Anna's face peered out. 'Did you want something?'

'Yes! I mean – n-no. Not exactly. I was just wondering . . . whether I could come in and watch you practise.'

I said it in this breathless rush, 'cos I was a bit embarrassed to tell you the truth. I don't know why I was embarrassed. I just was.

'You can watch,' said Anna, 'if you want to. But it's not very interesting. It's only barre work.'

'That's all right,' I said.

She opened the door to let me in. It felt really strange, walking into my bedroom and seeing all her stuff there. All her ballet pictures and her ballet books and the barre.

'Sit on the bed if you want,' said Anna.

She was wearing a leotard and tights and a pair of her pink ballet shoes. It made her look like a real proper dancer.

'It's only exercises,' she told me.

'I don't mind.'

I sat on the bed, my knees drawn up to my chin, watching as Anna did her *pliés* and her battermon tondew (which I now know is spelt *battement tendu*, but I didn't know it then).

'Do you want to see another sort of *battement*?' she said, after I'd been watching for about ten minutes. 'This is a *battement fondu*. It's to help you land safely. Watch!'

She stretched one leg out to the side and raised it into the air. Then she brought it down in front of her other leg, which had gone bendy at the knee. Next she straightened her bendy leg and stuck the other one straight out in front of her, with her arm (the one that wasn't holding on to the barre) curved over her head. It doesn't sound like anything particularly special, but the way Anna did it, it looked like a real dance step.

'Do you remember positions of the feet?' she said. '*First* position—'

She did that incredible thing, with her feet

all turned out in a straight line.

'Can anyone learn to do that?' I said.

'If they start early enough.'

'What's early enough?'

'Well . . . I should think eleven is the very *latest*. The younger you are, the better. I started when I was five.'

'But if someone started when they were eleven, they could still learn?'

'Mm . . . probably. Though not everyone has natural turn-out. And even if they have, not everyone ends up being a dancer. You have to have the right sort of body.'

I wondered if I had the right sort of body but didn't like to ask in case she said I hadn't.

'Can you do the splits?' I said.

'Everyone asks me that!'

I'd only asked because I knew that Sam could do them. But I didn't want to tell her that. And anyway, when Anna did them it was quite different. Sam was athletic, but Anna was graceful.

'Have you always wanted to be a dancer?' I said.

'Yes. Always,' said Anna; and she took hold of one foot under the instep and slowly extended her leg until it was way up above her head. She didn't do it to show off. She just did it like you might stretch your arms or wiggle your toes. Like it was perfectly natural.

'Right from when you were little?' I said.

'From when I was five years old.'

I could hardly believe it! Knowing what you wanted to do when you were *only five years old*. But I felt that she was telling me the truth.

'What would you do if you couldn't be a dancer?' I said.

Anna looked at me, puzzled, as if she didn't understand the question.

'Like, I want to be an interior designer,' I said. 'But if I can't be one, then I'd quite like to work with animals. What would you like to do? If you couldn't dance.'

A frown crinkled her forehead. 'There isn't

anything else. Dancing's the only thing I've ever wanted to do.'

'But suppose something happened?'

'Like what?'

'Well! Like you might grow too big, or something.'

Mary-Jo had told us that the girl she knew, the one who ate the carrots, had grown too big. That was *in spite of* eating the carrots. Now she was going to have to be a teacher, instead.

'Would you be a teacher?' I said.

Emphatically, Anna shook her head.

'Not until I'm too old to dance any more. Then I might be.'

'So what if you get too big?'

'I won't get too big! I've been measured. They can tell.'

'Well, but suppose you had an accident?'

It was silly, really, me keeping on like that. But I'd just never met anyone who was so sure of herself. Not even Sam. I mean, Sam knew what she wanted *now*; but not necessarily when she was grown up.

'I'm not going to have an accident,' said Anna. She sounded positive even about that!

'You mightn't be able to help it,' I said. 'You might be in a car crash.'

I wasn't trying to frighten her. I really wasn't! I was just trying to understand.

'You might get run over. You might be stricken by some incurable disease. Anything could happen!'

Anna looked at me out of her big dark eyes.

'Why are you doing this to me?' she said.

Of course I immediately felt terrible. Her nan had just died and here was I telling her how she might be run over or get a disease.

'I just think you have to be prepared,' I mumbled.

'But if I couldn't dance,' said Anna, 'I wouldn't want to go on living.'

She sounded like she really meant it. It was a little bit scary.

'Well, anyway,' I said, 'I don't expect any of it'll happen. I was just saying, what if.'

I went out on to the landing and peered over the banisters. I could hear that the television was on downstairs but I didn't feel like watching television. I thought that maybe I would see if I could do some painting in my new broom cupboardy bedroom. I knew that you were supposed to paint by natural light, but I guessed that if you were really dedicated you would be prepared to paint in any light that happened to be available. Even Anglepoise.

So I picked up my paint brush, but it wasn't any good. I didn't feel like painting, any more than I felt like watching television.

I opened the door of the titchy little spare room wardrobe and gazed at myself in the full-length mirror. Anna had said you had to have the right sort of body. Did I have the right sort of body? It wasn't terribly skinny, but it would probably get that way if I did as much practising as she did.

I left the wardrobe door open, so that I could watch myself, and using the edge of the chair as a barre I swooped down into a *plié*. Disaster! My heels *still* left the ground almost immediately, and in the mirror I could quite plainly see my bottom sticking up in the air. Anna's bottom hadn't stuck up. Her back had been straight and her bottom neatly tucked away out of sight. Not that she had much of a bottom.

That was because she practised all the time and burnt off the calories. Everyone had to start somewhere.

I decided that I would do *pliés* every night until I could do them like Anna.

'One, and – two, and – three, and—'

'Hey! Abi!'

The door burst open and Same came barging in.

'Do you mind?' I screamed, springing up and bashing my bum against the wardrobe door. 'That's very bad manners, that is!'

'It's only what you did to me the other day!' retorted Sam.

'That was 'cos I had something to tell you!'

'So I've got something to tell you ... *EastEnders* is on.'

'So what?' I rubbed at my bum. I was going to have the most enormous bruise.

'I thought you might want to watch it.'

'I'd have come down,' I said, 'if I'd wanted to watch it.'

'Oh, get her!' said Sam. 'She's all in a huff 'cos I caught her doing poncy ballet ... *again*!'

'I wasn't doing poncy ballet!'

'Looked like it to me,' said Sam. 'Knees *bend* ... bum *out* ... oops!' She cackled. 'I just laid an egg!'

'Well, don't go and scramble it over the carpet!' I said.

But I giggled, all the same. I couldn't help it.

4

We had this new routine, now that Anna was with us. Mum had to drive her into school every morning, then drive over again to pick her up at the end of the day. On Tuesdays, Wednesdays, Thursdays and Fridays she had ballet lessons, which meant Mum had to set off at five o'clock, leaving me and Sam to look after the Radish.

In some ways this was very inconvenient as we either had to rush up the road with the dogs and race round the park at breakneck speed in order to make sure we were back before Mum left; or else we had to drag the Radish with us. He was too little to be left in the house on his own, but he didn't always want to come for walks, he wanted to stay and watch telly, and if he couldn't he got all grizzly.

On Mondays, on the other hand, when Anna didn't have a ballet lesson, Mum had to leave at quarter past three to pick her up from school and we came home to an empty house. We didn't like that. We were used to Mum being there. We were used to our tea being on the table and Mum demanding to know what had happened at school – to which we usually replied 'Nothing' in an impatient tone of voice. Now, when she wasn't there, we missed her!

Sam grumbled about it. She said that Mum wasn't behaving like a proper mum any more.

'She's more like a private taxi service!'

'It's what happens when someone's dedicated,' I said.

'What, people have to run round after them?'

'Yes, because it's so important to them. It's something they *absolutely have to do*.'

Sam made one of her scoffing noises.

'Honestly!' I said. 'If ever you read about child prodigies, they've always had a mum or dad that devotes all their time to them. Like they take them to classes and make sure they have somewhere to practise and eat the right food, and all the family has to revolve around them and make sacrifices.'

Sam looked at me like she was going to be sick.

'That is disgusting!' she said.

'It's the only way they can be prodigies.'

'I don't care! It means they're only thinking about themselves. It's selfish!'

'Do you think Anna's selfish?'

'Yes, she is,' said Sam. 'She never says thank you! She just takes it all for granted.'

'She can't help it!' I felt this need to defend her. I don't know why. 'It's the way she's made . . . it's because of being dedicated.'

'Rats!' said Sam.

She wasn't at all sympathetic. I thought that it was because she hadn't taken the trouble to get to know Anna the way I had. Well, not *know*, exactly. Sometimes when a person is dedicated it's very hard to get to know them. They are so bound up in what they're doing they don't really notice other people. But I'd watched Anna doing her practice, I'd seen how hard she worked. I knew how much it meant to her.

'You're just making excuses,' said Sam.

'I'm not,' I said.

'Yes, you are! I bet Mum wouldn't take me to gym classes every day.'

'She probably would,' I said, 'if she thought that's what you really wanted to do.'

'Well, maybe it is what I really want to do!'

I looked at Sam, doubtfully.

'She wouldn't mind *taking* you,' I said, 'only I'm not sure we could afford it.'

'So how could I ever get to be a prodigy?' roared Sam. 'I thought you said a family had to make sacrifices?'

'Y-yes.' It was what I'd said. 'But they don't have to pay for Anna to have ballet lessons! Her dad pays.'

'And we all have to revolve round her!'

I didn't actually mind revolving round Anna. She was cool! She was so tiny and dainty and elegant. You never caught her doing anything clumping or ungainly. And I really admired the way she was so single-minded! I wouldn't ever have admitted it, not even to myself, but you could almost say she'd become a sort of role model.

It's kind of odd, I suppose, having a role model who's younger than you are, but in lots of ways Anna seemed far older than me and Sam. Her life already had a purpose: ours were just drifting. I mean, I knew that I wanted to go to art college one day, but art wasn't the *only* thing in my life. I did have other interests. Like just at this moment I was beginning to think I might be into ballet . . .

Of course I knew that however hard I tried I couldn't ever actually *be* a dancer. Probably. But I didn't see any reason I couldn't get to be like Anna! Just a little bit. If I stopped eating junk food and practised like mad, the way she did.

First off, I tied my hair in a pony tail, 'cos that's what Anna did with hers. Then I watched how she walked – straight-backed, with her head held high and her feet turned out – and started trying to walk the same way. It looked so graceful when Anna did it! There wasn't any call for Sam to scoff and say that I looked like a duck with a sore bum.

'You look like you've got something stuck up there!'

Sam can be *so* vulgar.

I decided to leave my feet to get on with it and just concentrate on the straight back and the head held high. The feet could come later, when I'd practised some more. I knew you couldn't expect them to start turning out all by themselves, overnight.

'Feet shouldn't turn out, anyway,' said Sam. 'It's not natural.'

'Neither's jumping in the air and turning double somersaults,' I retorted. That shut her up! Half the stuff Sam did in gym meant contorting her body into weird shapes. I mean, when was it ever natural to bend over backwards until your hands touched the ground? Or twist your legs behind your head, or do the splits?

Secretly I was trying to do the splits in my bedroom. My *broom* cupboard. I practised every evening before I went to bed. I reckoned that every evening I managed to stretch my legs just a little bit further. One of these days I was really going to surprise Sam!

As well as doing the splits I was practising positions of the feet and *pliés* and *battements*, just like Anna. I always put a chair against the bedroom door, in case Sam came marching in. I couldn't do all the stuff that Anna did because of the room being so small, and also because lots of it was too complicated; but I could wave my arms around if I stood on the bed, and I could put my legs up on the window sill and bend over the way she did.

I knew that Sam was far more athletic than I was, but Sam couldn't be a dancer! She liked playing football and going horse-riding. She'd end up with all these huge muscles in all the wrong places. And anyway, she was too tall. A whole lot taller than Anna. She'd grow too big! I wouldn't. I'm quite a small sort of person. All I had to do was practise – and cut down on the cheese-and-onion crisps!

It just so happens that I adore cheese-and-onion crisps. I also rather like chips and chocolate. But I didn't seem to be built in quite the same way Anna was. She could eat whatever she wanted and still be sparrow-like. But I'd read about people suffering for their art, and I thought most likely the suffering would include not eating the things you most enjoyed.

I had to keep making up excuses 'cos I didn't want Mum or Sam to know what I was doing. Sam would have jeered and Mum would have told me not to be so silly. She'd have said, 'It's good to eat sensibly, but you're a growing girl! A few treats now and again won't hurt you.'

Mum is a great one for treats, and so am I, as a rule. It was a real struggle to say no when some of my favourite goodies turned up.

'I just don't feel like it,' I'd say, when in fact

there was nothing I felt like more. Or, 'I'm not really very hungry,' when I was utterly ravenous. And all the time I had to watch Sam and Anna eating away like mad, with neither of them putting on so much as an ounce, and it was *agony*. But I kept at it 'cos I'd tested my thighs the way Mary-Jo had tested hers, I'd sat on the edge of a chair and looked at the way they flobbed. Ugh! Horrible! Anna's didn't flob.

Sam's didn't, either, which was just plain annoying. I mean, when you consider the way she stuffed herself with junk food. There are times when life can be distinctly unfair.

But then one day I found that I could actually pull the tape measure *really tight* round my waist without having great rolls of flab come squidging out on either side of it. Hurray! A moment of victory! Now I only had tiny weeny little rolls that you could just about pinch between finger and thumb.

I felt really triumphant! Next day, when Mum had gone to fetch Anna, and Sam and the Radish were downstairs, I crept into Anna's bedroom and helped myself to one of her leotards and a pair of her trousers and went guiltily scurrying off to my broom cupboard to try them on – putting the chair against the door first, you can bet!

I tried the trousers first. But guess what? I couldn't even get them done up! I struggled and wriggled and held in my tummy as hard as I could go, but still there was this great gap with all my horrible pinky flesh bulging out. Ugh! Ugh! Ugh! It made me feel sick.

I peeled the trousers off and put the leotard on. I gazed at myself in the wardrobe mirror. I couldn't believe it! What I saw was this little roly poly person with a round chubby face and dimpled knees. I'm not kidding! My knees had *dimples*.

It was a bitter disappointment. But I was determined not to give up! I would simply go on an even stricter sort of diet. I told Mum, for instance, that milk made me feel ill ('cos I'd heard that milk was fattening) so she got me this skimmed stuff that tasted like washing-up water. Then I started having marge instead of butter on my toast 'cos I utterly and absolutely *loathe* marge. But that way I only had the merest scraping. When I have butter, I whop it on in huge great dollops.

Mum did get a bit hot and bothered when I stopped eating butter. She said, 'What's wrong with you? You're not going off your food, are you?'

I said, 'Mum, marge is *healthier*.'

'Well – yes, all right, I suppose so,' said Mum. 'But I don't want you getting faddy!'

At school in the canteen I ate stuff like vegetables and fruit. A teacher saw me carrying my tray over to a table one day and said, 'Good girl! Healthy living. I wish there were a few more like you.'

Sam said I was mad. She said, 'What's your game? Are you getting anorexic?'

'I'm just trying to be healthy,' I said, looking pointedly at her plate of chips.

'You're behaving like that girl,' said Mary-Jo. 'That one I told you about . . . she used to eat like that. She was all skin and bone.'

'Abi's not skin and bone,' said Lissie. She leaned across the table and poked me with a finger. 'She's like a jam doughnut!'

Everybody giggled.

'She'll *get* all skin and bone,' said Sam, 'if she carries on like that.'

I did my best to ignore them. I was sure that this was what Anna would have done. All Anna cared about was her dancing. She didn't care about stupid people and their stupid jibes. I was going to be like Anna!

Unfortunately, at home, we don't have any bathroom scales. Mum says it's not good to become obsessed with your weight. She says if you have scales in the house you spend your life jumping on and off them, counting the kilos. So I didn't really have any way to check whether my new healthy-living diet was working or not. All I could do was keep measuring myself and pinching at the rolls of fat, until one day . . . there weren't any! I pulled the tape as tight as it would go. I turned sideways. I wasn't roly poly any more! I'd got a shape! I was getting like Anna!

I waited for someone to remark on it, but nobody did. Not even Mum. Nobody said to me, 'You're looking nice and slim these days, Abi.' They were all so used to me being chubby that they just assumed I still was. Your family is always the last to notice these things.

But I noticed! I noticed that I could bend and stretch without great bubbles of flesh billowing out of me. One Saturday I went into the shopping centre by myself, *without Sam*, and bought a leotard. A white one, like Anna's. And when I put it on and looked at myself sideways in the mirror, joy of joys! My big pobbly tummy had disappeared! Well, almost disappeared. It wasn't quite like Anna's, which actually caved *in*; but at least I didn't look like a pregnant garden gnome (which was what a particularly horrible girl at school, Lauren Babcock, had once called me, under the impression she was being funny).

Next day, which was Sunday, Sam wanted me

to go up the park with her and practise passing. She was dead set on getting into the Under-Thirteen netball team.

'I can't,' I said. 'I've got things to do.'

'What things?' said Sam.

'Just things,' I said. As a matter of fact I was going to go back to the shopping centre and buy a pair of ballet shoes. Pink, like Anna's. But I wasn't telling Sam!

She was quite put out.

'Why are you being so secretive?' she said. 'What are you up to?'

I said, 'I'm not up to anything. I suppose a person is allowed a bit of privacy?'

'Are you meeting someone?' said Sam. 'You haven't got a *boy*friend?'

'No, I have not!' I said.

'So why can't you come and practise with me?'

' 'Cos I told you! I've got things to do. Ask Anna.'

'*Anna.*' Sam said it contemptuously. 'She wouldn't come!'

'She might if you asked her.'

' 'Course she wouldn't! She'll be up in her room, prinking and prancing.'

Sam prinked and pranced, being Anna.

'She doesn't look like that,' I said.

'Yes, she does! She *points* her lickle toes and she *waves* her lickle arms . . . if you won't come,' said Sam, 'I shall go up the road and ask Mary-Jo!'

I hesitated. I didn't like Sam doing things with Mary-Jo, without me; but I *did* want those ballet shoes! Now that I was no longer roly poly.

'All right,' said Sam. 'I shall ask Mary-Jo!'

Sam went flouncing off while I went upstairs to raid my savings. I'd really been saving up for some proper oil paints, but just at that moment the ballet shoes seemed more important.

As I passed Anna's room I heard the sound of music and knew that she was practising. I had to get those ballet shoes, then I could practise, too! Maybe we could practise together. I wasn't as

70

advanced as Anna, of course. Nowhere near. But I could catch up!

I went zooming into town, full of these great plans about how I'd ask Mum if I could have ballet lessons. I had to do it *now*, while I was still young enough. If I left it till I was twelve, it would be too late!

Sam would jeer, of course. I decided I'd tell her it was for my ankles. Anna had said that was the reason some people were sent to ballet, if they had weak ankles and wanted to strengthen them. I'd say that Miss Betts, our PE teacher, had told me. I could already hear the imaginary conversation I'd had with her.

'Your ankles are rather weak, Abi! Why don't you ask your mother if you can have some ballet lessons, to strengthen them?'

'Oh, I will, Miss Betts! What a good idea!'

And then I'd tell Sam that I didn't actually *want* to do ballet. I just thought that I ought, because of my ankles. That way she couldn't jeer. You don't jeer at people who have physical defects.

In the shopping centre there's a shop called The Dance Emporium. I don't quite know what an emporium is, I think perhaps it just means a big shop, but the Dance Emporium sold everything to do with dance. I felt a bit shy about going in and asking for a pair of pink ballet shoes. I thought the lady who served me would know at once that I wasn't really a dancer. But she didn't! She said, 'Blocked or unblocked?' Just like I'd been learning ballet for ever and ever!

I said, 'Unblocked, please.' And then, remembering what Anna had told me: 'I haven't gone on to my points yet.'

'Oh, wait till you do!' she said. 'It'll be very exciting!'

I wondered how long it would take. I would have loved to buy some blocked shoes right there and then and go up on my toes, but I thought maybe I'd better not. Not if I was serious. Which I was!

I rushed home with my beautiful pink shoes

and some lengths of satin ribbon I'd bought to sew on to them. I'd looked very closely at Anna's, and I knew just how to do it. I knew where to place the ribbons. I knew how to tie them, crossed over, round the ankle, with the ends neatly tucked in. When I put them on, and got into my leotard, with my hair pulled back into a knot (the way Anna did hers when she practised) I felt that I looked like a real dancer. Me! Abi! Who ever would have thought it?

It's what one of our teachers at junior school used to say: 'You never know until you try.'

I practised all afternoon in my new pink shoes! I did the *pliés* and the *battements* and positions of the feet. (I still couldn't turn out in a straight line the way Anna did, but I imagined all my tendons and my muscles stretching themselves a little bit more each day.) I did arm positions and things called *developpés* and other things called *croisés*. I was learning lots of French!

By the time Mum called me down to supper I was dead hungry, but it was cheese sandwiches and I'd read somewhere that cheese was nothing but great gobbets of fat, so I suffered for my art and only ate one.

'Surely you're going to have more than that?' said Mum. She hates it when people don't eat.

I shook my head. 'I'm full up,' I said.

Sam looked at me darkly across the table. *She'd* eaten three. So had Anna.

'How can you be full up?' Mum wanted to know.

'I just am.'

'She's bats,' said Sam, stuffing her mouth with sandwich.

One night on television we watched this old movie called *Saturday Night Fever*, which Mum and Dad said took them right back.

'Look! Can you imagine?' said Mum. 'That's the kind of dancing we used to do then!'

'What, you and Dad?' I said.

I could hardly believe it! Mum and Dad all dressed up and leaping about?

'Oh, we've been young in our time,' said Mum.

I shook my head.

'It's great!' said Sam.

'It's only people jumping about,' I said.

I suppose, really, I was trying to impress Anna. 'Cos I thought she would agree with me and turn up her nose. I was surprised when she agreed with Sam and said that John Travolta, who was the star, was 'a really good dancer'.

'It's not like ballet,' I said.

'That's *right*,' said Sam. 'It's not all p—'

I could see that she was about to say 'poncy'. She stopped herself just in time.

'There's all different kinds of dancing,' said Anna. 'Ballet's only one.'

'But ballet's best,' I said.

'It's just different,' said Anna.

'See?' Sam mouthed it at me.

Next day, which was Sunday, we were all out in the garden, including Anna. She was reading one of her ballet books, Sam and me were messing around with the dogs, Mum and Dad were sitting in deck chairs saying how lovely and warm it was for the time of year. The Radish was whingeing that he was bored.

'Abi! Tham!' He tugged at our sleeves. 'Play wiv me! I'm bored!'

I wonder if I got bored when I was only seven? Maybe I did. I don't remember.

'Play wiv me!' screeched the Radish.

'Don't be so tetchy,' I said.

'Play wiv me, play wiv me!' The Radish pummelled at my arm. Honestly! He never used to do that when he first came to us. He was starting to behave like a real *boy*.

'I know what we'll do!' Sam jumped up. 'We'll have a disco! Like in the film. I'll go and put some music on!'

'Not too loud,' warned Mum. 'Think of the neighbours!'

But old Mrs Tizzard on one side is deaf, and horrid Mrs Pink on the other side was away visiting her daughter, so it didn't really matter.

'Dance, dance!' commanded Sam, running back into the garden.

The sounds of music drifted out through the French windows. I recognised it as Mum's *Greatest Hits From the 70s* CD that Dad had given her for her birthday. Just like the music in the film!

'I'm grooving!' cried Sam. She grabbed hold of the Radish's hand. 'Groove with me, baby! Everyone join in!'

Mum and Dad laughed, but got up from their deck chairs. I hesitated just at first, feeling suddenly shy, but then I saw that Anna was on her feet and so I thought if she could do it, so could I, and soon we were all disco dancing, all around the garden.

Mum and Dad pretty soon gave up – 'A bit too old for this sort of thing,' said Dad – but the rest of us carried on. I danced with Anna, while Sam danced with the Radish. The Radish couldn't really dance; he just bounced around. I knew that if Mrs Tizzard had her window open and was looking out, it would be me and Anna she was watching.

I felt like a star! I felt like I was on stage! I was dancing with Anna, like I was just as good as she was. Like I was a real proper dancer. And I wasn't roly poly any more!

All the rest of the day I was flushed with triumph (as the saying goes). Mum and Dad's verdict had been, 'Brilliant! A real floor show!'

'We seem to have a whole houseful of little dancers,' beamed Mum.

But I knew she couldn't mean Sam and the Radish. She was only including them to be kind.

That night, after we'd gone to bed – well, after me and Sam and Anna had gone to bed – I came creeping back downstairs for something to eat. I was just so hungry! I seemed to be hungry most of the time these days. Healthy food didn't seem to fill you up quite as much as the unhealthy sort. It didn't always taste as good, either. *Nothing* tastes as good as cheese-and-onion crisps! But one has to suffer for one's art.

I stole down the stairs really quietly and trod on tiptoe past the sitting-room 'cos I didn't want

Mum to catch me at it. The sitting-room door was ajar and I could hear Dad's voice.

'I enjoyed that, this afternoon . . . a really nice little show. It's good to see the kids amusing themselves instead of just sitting in front of the telly.'

'It's funny, though, isn't it,' said Mum, 'how Anna's the one you have to watch?'

'She's a great little mover,' agreed Dad. 'Mind you, our Sam's not so bad.'

'No, she's not,' said Mum. 'I reckon she could make a dancer, if she wanted.'

'Put the two of them together and they'd be really cracking!'

I didn't bother going into the kitchen after that. I suddenly didn't feel hungry any more. I felt quite sick and trembly.

I fled back upstairs and into bed. Why hadn't they noticed me? Why *hadn't* they?

I knew they didn't mean it, but there are times when your mum and dad can be ever so hurtful.

5

I was in the garden next morning – it was Monday, but it was half-term – watching Anna do her centre practice. Centre practice was when she came away from the barre and did things without anything to hold on to. Things like *arabesques* and *fouettés*. *Arabesques* were standing on one leg with the other stretched out behind. *Fouettés* were spinning round like a top.

'And this is a *pirouette*,' said Anna; but even I knew what a pirouette was.

I hunched on the branch of the apple tree, the one me and Sam used as our own private sitting-place, and carefully took note of all the details. *Pirouettes* looked a bit too complicated, and so did *fouettés*, but I thought I could manage an *arabesque* all right. And the jumping thing, the *jeté*.

A *jeté* looked easy. Just a little spring into the

air and down again on to one foot. I was sure I could do that! If I could just have the garden to myself for a while . . .

I was too shy to try it in front of Anna. It would be so embarrassing if I did it wrong! And anyway, I didn't want her to know that I was secretly copying her. It's quite belittling, when you're eleven years old, to be secretly copying someone who's only ten. But Anna wasn't like a ten-year-old! When me and Sam had been ten, we'd spent most of our time giggling and telling silly jokes and thinking it was really daring to say words like boob or bra, even though it had usually made me go bright tomato. I had gone bright tomato a *lot* when I was ten.

Actually, I still did. Sometimes I think perhaps I have an overactive blood supply to the face, and that's why I keep blushing all the time. I wish I didn't!

Anna never blushed. She almost never giggled. She didn't tell silly jokes. In that respect, she was a bit like a nun. I don't expect nuns ever do any of those things. A nun has no room in her life for anything but God: Anna had no room in her life for anything except ballet.

I'd said this to Sam one day when she was carrying on, but Sam had only made a rude noise and said, '*Boring!*'

But Anna wasn't boring! She was fascinating – especially when she was doing her ballet. I just loved to watch her! I loved the way her arms curved and her legs unfolded, slowly, like the petals of a flower opening up. I loved her poise and her daintiness and the tilt of her head on her neck, which was long and slender.

I'd never thought to notice anyone's neck before. Now I looked at necks all the time! In the street, on the bus, in assembly. I'd discovered that most people had quite *short* necks. Some had great thick red ones, all bulging out over their collars. Others were rather thin and wobbly. But Anna's was like a swan's. It was so graceful!

I didn't try saying this to Sam as I knew she would only make fun of me. Sam isn't an artist;

she doesn't see things the way I do.

Anna had stopped practising and was wiping herself dry with a towel.

'That's enough for today,' she said. 'It's important to know when to stop.'

She sounded so grown up!

'Yes,' I said. And I nodded, trying to sound grown up myself. 'It wouldn't be good to overdo things.'

She came and perched next to me, on the branch of the apple tree. We sat for a while in silence. I swung my legs to and fro, but Anna just sat perfectly still. She was one of those people, she could sit for ages without moving. I always get a twitch or an itch and start wriggling, but with Anna, it was like she was made out of – not stone. That's too hard – something delicate and precious such as . . . porcelain!

Mum has an ornament made out of porcelain that she inherited from Auntie Marge (who also left us the house). It is very very beautiful and worth quite a lot of money, so that Mum keeps it locked away in a glass-fronted cabinet where Felix, our cat, cannot get at it.

I suddenly had this fantastical notion that Anna could be kept in a glass-fronted cabinet! I almost wished I had my paints there, so I could do a portrait of her.

The silence went on. I pictured Anna in her cabinet, standing in a corner of the room. Then I thought that perhaps she could be one of those little figures that you get on the tops of musical boxes. When the music starts playing, the figure starts dancing. It's usually a ballerina in a sticky-out skirt.

I swung my legs more vigorously, and the branch swayed slightly beneath us. Silence bothers me! It doesn't seem natural, two people sitting together without talking. I racked my brains for something to say.

'This tree has really good apples,' I said.

'Does it?' said Anna. Silence didn't seem to bother her.

'Yes, it does,' I said. 'All crisp and juicy. If

the birds don't get them first!'

Anna smiled slightly, but she didn't say anything. She wasn't at all an easy sort of person to talk to. If that had been Sam sitting there, we'd have been chattering away like mad.

'Dad wrote out this notice one time and pinned it on the bird table . . . PLEASE DON'T EAT OUR APPLES. But they didn't take any notice,' I said.

'Perhaps they can't read,' said Anna.

She looked at me, very solemnly. I *suppose* she was making a joke.

'They're very ungrateful,' I said. 'Dad says they're some of the best-fed birds in the neighbourhood. We give them proper bird seed, and we give them bacon rind, and nut bags . . . you'd think they could leave the apples alone.'

'You'd think so,' said Anna.

'We feed the foxes, as well,' I said. 'We have a whole family that comes here.'

Surely that would get her going? A family of foxes!

'What do they eat?' said Anna.

'Dog food, mostly. And the hedgehogs, too! We give them dog food.'

'I thought hedgehogs liked bread and milk.'

'No, dog food's best.'

Anna stretched out a leg, and pointed her toe. Another silence descended.

'You know all these exercises you do,' I said. 'Do all dancers have to do them?'

'Yes. Even prima ballerinas.'

'What's a prima ballerina?'

'They're the leading dancers in a company.'

'And they have to do all the stuff you do?'

'Every day,' said Anna. 'All their lives.'

'Even when they're old?'

'So long as they're still dancing. If you don't practise, your muscles grow stiff.'

'Don't you ever get bored?' I said.

Anna shook her head. 'If I got bored, I wouldn't do it.'

I wondered if I would get bored. I had a horrible feeling that I probably would.

'You must be really dedicated,' I said.

'You have to be,' agreed Anna.

There was a pause. I wondered what else to talk about.

'I'm dedicated,' I said.

'Are you?' said Anna.

'Yes! I'm dedicated to art. I'm going to go to art school when I'm old enough. I'm going to be an interior designer.'

'Really?' said Anna. But she didn't sound terribly interested. I got the feeling she was just saying it to be polite.

'P'raps you don't know what an interior designer is?' I said. Lots of people don't.

'What is it?' said Anna.

'It's someone who plans the insides of people's houses for them. Like what colour wallpaper to have, and what sort of carpet, and what sort of lights. Only they don't just do it for houses. They can do it for anything! Theatres or restaurants or – or even palaces!' I said. 'And then they'd be *By Appointment*. To Her Majesty,'

I added, in case she didn't understand.

Well! I thought she might be just a little bit impressed, but she didn't show any signs of it. She was a *really* difficult person to have a conversation with! The only subject that made her come to life was ballet. Maybe it was the only thing she knew about, 'cos as far as I could make out she didn't have any other interests. And she didn't seem to have any special friends at school, either, or if she did she never mentioned them. But I didn't really see how she could have. It was like she lived in her own little private bubble and no one else could get in.

I remembered Sam saying that she was selfish. I didn't think that, exactly. Not *selfish*. Just incredibly single-minded. Some people are made that way; they can't help it. They have this very powerful force inside them that drives them on. I wasn't blaming Anna. But I couldn't help thinking what a lot of havoc it caused in other people's lives.

I mean, there was me turned out of my

bedroom and living in a broom cupboard, and there was Mum rushing to and fro, taking her to school and picking her up. Mum must be worn to a frazzle! 'Cos she didn't only have Anna to think of (though sometimes, just lately, that was the way it seemed). She had me and Sam and the Radish; and Dad and the dogs and Felix. She had the shopping to do and the house to keep clean and the meals to prepare and Dad's accounts to see to and the telephone to answer and appointments to make when people wanted plumbing jobs done.

It suddenly occurred to me that Mum must have been mad, saying we'd take Anna! And maybe I'd been mad, too, saying I'd go and live in a broom cupboard. Why had we done it??? No one had made us! I thought that perhaps this was what happened when people were single-minded. Everyone falls under their spell and offers to do things for them. Not that Dad or Sam had. Dad couldn't, because Dad had to get on with his plumbing; and Sam hadn't because Sam isn't the sort of person to fall under anyone's spell. But me and Mum had been well and truly mesmerised!

Anna slid down off the branch.

'I think I'll go in, now,' she said.

'Yes, all right,' I said.

I watched her walk back up the garden with her ballet dancer's walk that I'd tried so hard to copy. Mum and Dad and the Radish were all indoors. Sam was round at Mary-Jo's, practising her netball. I was on my own!

I sprang down and took up a position in the middle of the grass, just like Anna had. Positions of the feet . . . positions of the arms . . . In my head, I could hear Anna chanting them.

'*En avant . . . à la seconde . . . bras croisé . . .*'

I couldn't remember the others! There was one where you held your arms above your head, and one where you held one up and one out to the side, but I couldn't remember what they were called.

I tried an arabesque. It looked so easy when

Anna did it! One arm stretched out before you, one arm behind. Head high, straight back. Balance on one l-l-l—

As usual, I wobbled. I tried it again, holding on to the branch of the apple tree. If I bent my top halfway down I could raise one leg behind me almost as high as Anna could. But Anna didn't bend her top half! She kept it upright. My back didn't seem stretchy enough.

I was still bending and wobbling and trying to stay upright when Sam appeared round the side of the house.

'Ho ho ho!' she cried, bouncing her netball at me. 'You'd never make a dancer!'

I knew she wasn't saying it to be deliberately hurtful. She wasn't to know that I'd turned Anna into my role model. Sam's always teasing me about being clumsy and tripping over my own feet. It's sort of a family joke.

'Watch out, Abi's about!'

'Batten down the hatches!'

'Abi's got two left feet!'

Why do people do this to people? I didn't tease Sam about not being able to draw or paint. I didn't say to her, 'Ho ho ho! You'd never make an artist' or tell her that she'd got two left hands.

Even if I had, she wouldn't care. *She* wouldn't turn bright scarlet, like some kind of human strawberry.

'What were you trying to do?' said Sam. 'Standing on one leg like a stork!'

'It's called an arabesque,' I said.

Sam immediately swooped down with one leg stuck up in the air.

'Nothing to it!'

'You're not supposed to bend over,' I said, sourly. 'You're supposed to stay upright.'

'Like this?'

You'll never believe it . . . she did an almost perfect arabesque! Almost as good as Anna.

'I could be a dancer if I wanted,' she said.

I knew that this was probably true.

'But you wouldn't want to be,' I urged. ''Cos it's poncy!'

'Mm . . .' Sam stopped, and seemed to consider it. 'It's not as poncy as I thought.'

'But you wouldn't want to get all dressed up in girly things! Ballet shoes and sticky-out skirts and—'

'Tutus,' said Sam.

'What?'

'Tutus. It's what they're called.'

'How do you know?'

'I know all sorts of things!' said Sam; and she twizzled round in a pirouette. 'Bet you don't know how to do this without getting dizzy!'

'How?' I said, rather reluctantly.

' 's easy! You just fix your eyes on something . . . like this.' Sam squinted fiercely at the bird table. 'Then you make sure your head goes round *faster*—' she whipped her head round – 'than your body! Keep on all day that way.'

It was very disheartening. I tried it after Sam had gone indoors but I only had to twizzle round once and I got dizzy. How was it Sam could do these things and not me? It was so unfair! I'd practised and practised.

I tried reminding myself that Sam couldn't draw for toffee, she couldn't even draw a black cat in the dark; but it wasn't very much comfort.

I trailed indoors feeling like a pathetic insignificant nobody.

6

Tuesday morning, and for all the rest of the week, Anna had special half-term ballet classes. They were instead of her evening ones. They started at ten o'clock and went right through till half-past twelve.

'Two-and-a-half solid hours of class!' marvelled Mum.

'Some of it's rehearsal,' said Anna, 'for the end-of-term show. And some of it's for the competition. Miss Heriot wants to make sure I'm ready for it.'

She was going in for this Young Dancer competition. If she won, it meant they would pay her fees when she started full-time at ballet school. I could see that it was important, but I did feel a bit resentful. I tried not to; I really did. But I just couldn't help it!

Even at half-term Mum was going to be

whizzing about, transporting Anna. You'd have thought, at ten years old, she could have been trusted to get herself there and back. It wasn't as if she was a *young* ten years old. Dad had said only the other day that she had more sense than me and Sam put together.

Cheek! Just because we'd tried tobogganing down the stairs on a tea tray and knocked a chunk out of the wall. We'd read in a book about people going down the stairs on a tea tray. How were we to know it wouldn't work? You'd think if you'd read it in a book it would be OK.

The only reason Anna hadn't done it was 'cos she was scared of hurting herself. I suppose that could be called sensible. But dead boring!

Anyway. I'd suggested to Mum that she ought to be left to go by bus, but Mum had said a very firm *no*.

'I'm responsible for her. If anything happened it would be my fault.'

I said, 'What could happen? Between here and there?'

'She's only ten,' said Mum.

'But she's so *sensible*,' I said.

All Mum could think to say to that was, 'Abi, don't argue with me.'

She didn't seem to care about polluting the atmosphere. *Or* about leaving the rest of us in the house on our own. I mean, anything could have happened! Suppose burglars broke in? Suppose the Radish set light to his wastepaper basket and burned the place to a cinder? I'd caught him only the other day playing with a box of matches in his bedroom. How would Mum feel then? If she came back to find nothing but blackened ruins and grisly skeletons that were her children?

'I'd feel,' said Mum, when I put it to her, 'that someone hadn't been keeping an eye on Gus as they ought.'

Well! I ask you. What a thing to say! Any normal mum would have been in floods of tears even just thinking about it.

But Mum wasn't normal, these days. It was

like she'd been hypnotised. Like Anna, all of a sudden, was Little Miss Perfect. Mum went on and on, that morning at breakfast, about how dedicated Anna was. How she'd never known anyone so single-minded. How *unusual* it was for someone so young to be so determined.

'You're really set on going to ballet school, aren't you?'

'I'm really set on going to art school,' I said.

'Since when?' said Sam.

'Since ages!' I said.

It's really terrible, the way no one ever listens to you. Mum certainly didn't. She just carried on like I'd never even spoken.

'You work so hard! I really thought they'd let you have a rest at half term.'

'I'm not having a rest,' I said. 'I'm g—'

'All work and no play,' said Mum.

'I'm g—'

'Still, I suppose if you're going in for this competition—'

'I'm going in for a competition!' I shouted.

I shouted it so loud that Jack jumped up and started barking.

'Jack, be quiet!' said Mum. She looked at me. At last! '*You're* going in for a competition?'

'Well, I might be,' I said. 'I've got to go in this morning and find out.'

'Go in where?'

'School!'

'This morning? You're going in *this morning*?'

Well! At least I'd got Mum's attention.

I nodded, proudly. 'It's the Summer Art competition. There's six of us and Mr Martin's going to tell us the ones he's putting in for it.'

'Why didn't you tell me before?' wailed Mum. 'I've arranged a dentist's appointment! Who's going to look after Gus?'

It was all she cared about. She didn't care about me going in for an art competition. (Maybe. If I got chosen.) She only cared about who was going to look after the Radish!

'I can't.' Sam said it quickly. 'I'm going riding.'

'Yes, I know you're going riding,' said Mum. 'I

99

knew about that. You told me. Abi didn't mention a thing about going in to school!'

'I tried to,' I said.

It was true. I'd tried to tell Mum on Friday afternoon when I got home but she'd been too busy to listen. Either she'd been on the computer, bashing away at an urgent job for Dad, or else she'd been on the phone talking to people about plumbing jobs; and then when she'd finally got off the computer and the phone had stopped ringing, it had been time for her to go and pick Anna up. And after that, I'd forgotten.

'Can't have tried very hard,' said Sam.

'I did! But Mum's always in such a rush.'

'Abi, do you *have* to go in?' said Mum. 'Couldn't you just ring up?'

'No! If I'm chosen he'll want to talk about it.'

'Well, ring up and find out.'

'*No.*' I wriggled on my chair. The thought of ringing school and asking to speak to Mr Martin made me feel embarrassed. I don't like speaking on the telephone. Specially not about things that matter. Specially not to a *teacher*.

'Oh, Abi!' Mum tutted, impatiently. 'This is very inconvenient! Now what am I going to do?'

'You could always make another appointment,' I said.

'But he fitted me in specially! I've lost a filling, I need it seen to!'

I pursed my lips and prodded up and down with my spoon in my cereal bowl. I knew Mum was waiting for me to give in and say that I would stay home and look after the Radish for her, but I wasn't going to! I'd already given up my bedroom and was living in a broom cupboard. I wasn't going to miss out on my big chance! For all I knew, if I didn't go in to school Mr Martin wouldn't choose me. And all of a sudden, I desperately wanted him to. Mum hadn't looked at me twice when I was disco dancing; but if I got chosen for the art competition she would have to sit up and take notice. She couldn't not!

'Take the Radish with you,' I said. I turned, very firmly, to the Radish. 'You wouldn't mind going with Mum, would you? You could sit in the waiting-room and read a nice comic. You'd enjoy it, you'd—'

'No!' The Radish screamed and splattered his spoon on top of his Crunchy Pops. 'Not going! Not going!'

'They're not going to do anything to you,' I said. 'It's for Mum. It's—'

'Not! Not!'

The Radish was whipping himself up into one of his frenzies.

'Now see what you've done,' said Sam.

'Not going! Not going! Not going!'

I sighed. It wasn't the Radish's fault. He was very badly treated by one of his mum's boyfriends before he came to us and it's left him with scars. There are all kinds of things he's terrified of. Going to the dentist is just one of them. Last time Mum had taken him he'd screamed the place down.

But I still wasn't going to give in!

'Well, I shall obviously have to cancel, shan't

I?' said Mum. And she gave me this really venomous look as she went out to the hall to ring the dentist.

'Poor Mum,' said Sam. 'If she gets toothache it will be all your fault.'

'Won't,' I said. 'She should have listened when I tried to tell her. If she wasn't always so *busy*—' I shot this glance across the table at Anna. I wasn't exactly blaming Anna; but I did think she ought to be made aware. 'If she wasn't so busy, she might have heard me!'

Considering that just a few weeks ago it had been Sam who was grumbling like mad about Mum never being here, and not behaving like a proper mum, you'd have thought she'd have backed me up. But did she? No! She turned on me.

'You had all weekend to tell her! She wasn't busy all weekend! I mean, just springing it on her like that at the last moment,' said Sam, all smug and virtuous. 'Cos she'd told Mum about her horse-riding days ago, hadn't she? With Sam's loud voice, not even Mum could avoid hearing.

'It slipped my memory,' I said, with cold dignity. 'I can't be expected to remember *everything*.'

'You'd think you could if it's as earth-shattering as you make out!'

I suppose the truth, it hadn't seemed particularly earth-shattering when Mr Martin had first told us. I'd just thought, then, that it would be quite nice if I were chosen. But that was before we'd done the disco dancing. Before I'd overheard Mum and Dad talking about it. Saying how Anna was the one you had to watch, but how 'our Sam' wasn't so bad.

'*She could make a dancer, if she wanted.*'

They hadn't even noticed me!

Mum came back into the room.

'All right,' she said. 'I'm going next week. It's the soonest they can fit me in.'

She didn't actually *say* 'So I hope my tooth lasts out until then,' but I knew that was what she was thinking.

After breakfast, when Sam had gone off to her

horse-riding and Mum had gone off with the Radish to drive Anna to her class, I began to feel a bit guilty. Not *hugely* guilty, because I did think Mum ought to have listened; but a little bit guilty, in case she got toothache. So to make up for it, before I left, I vacuumed the hall and polished the hall table till it shone. It was more than Sam had done. Sam hadn't done anything!

School felt very strange and ghostly without the usual hordes of people cluttering up the corridors. In fact it felt quite scary, so that I was really glad when I reached the art studio and found Mr Martin waiting for me. The others were already there. They had already heard the good news: we were all being put in for the competition! But I was the only one from my year, so that made me feel a bit special.

We spent the morning going through what Mr Martin called our portfolios, meaning all the artwork we'd done in school that term, and discussing what subjects we might tackle for the competition. I went tearing jubilantly back home to tell Mum about it.

'Mum, Mum!' I yelled, bursting through the kitchen door. 'Guess what? I've been chosen!'

'Have you?' said Mum. 'That's good. That'll make my toothache more bearable!'

I knew she was only joking, but I wished she hadn't said it.

'Did you see I vacuumed the hall?' I said, anxiously.

'Yes, I did. Thank you! I appreciated that.'

'And I polished the table?'

'Yes, I noticed.'

'I'm the only person from my year to be chosen,' I said.

'Really?' said Mum.

'We have to do a drawing or a painting on our own. Not school work. I thought—' I dodged out of the way as Mum went racing past. 'I thought maybe I'd do a picture of Jack. Or maybe Felix. Which do you—' I dodged again – 'think would be better?'

'Oh, Abi, I don't know!'

Mum tore distractedly from one side of the kitchen to the other.

'Cats are so lovely,' I said. 'But I'm not sure about the colour.' Felix is pure white. 'It'd be more interesting if he was a tabby, or—'

'Abi, talk to me later, pet! I can't listen right now.' Mum snatched up a tea towel and threw it down again. 'Where are the car keys? What have I done with the car keys?'

'Here,' I said, taking them out of the vegetable rack. 'I suppose I could always *make* him a tabby. I could find a ph—'

'Gus!' Mum stuck her head out into the hallway. 'I'm going to pick Anna up. Are you coming?'

'A photograph,' I said.

'What?' Mum looked at me, perplexed. 'What photograph?'

'I could always find one! To copy.'

'Yes, why not? That would be lovely. Now, listen, after I've picked Anna up we're going to do a bit of shopping. She needs some new shoes and while I'm there I thought I'd see if I could find myself something to wear for Dad's do.'

Mum and Dad had been invited to attend a special dinner party. Mum was in quite a flap over it.

'An *evening* dress?' I said.

'Well – yes. I suppose it will have to be.'

'I'll come with you!'

I wasn't having Mum buy herself a new dress without me being there to supervise!

'Come on, then,' said Mum. 'Let's get going!'

Sam appeared just as we were climbing into the car. When she heard that we were going to buy Mum an evening dress she decided that she wanted to come, too – 'Otherwise you'll get something dowdy!' – and immediately climbed into the back next to me in her tatty old sweatshirt and horsey jeans, with her boots all covered in muck.

'You can't come shopping like that!' I screeched.

That dreadful girl! Guess what she did? She

took out her *handkerchief*. She cleaned her boots with her *handkerchief*. Horsey people are so disgusting!

Before going to buy Mum's evening dress we had to drive across town to pick Anna up. I'd never seen her dancing school before. Once upon a time – say, a day or two ago – I'd have been consumed with vulgar curiosity. I'd have wanted to read the brass plate on the door and go up the steps and look inside. Now, somehow, it didn't really interest me very much. I don't know why. I just wanted to get to the shopping centre and help Mum choose her dress.

In the car I tried bringing up the subject of Felix again, and whether I should turn him into a tabby, but Mum was busy negotiating roadworks and Sam was busy telling us how she'd been over her first jump. How it was a *real* jump, and how she'd got this amazingly wonderful seat and how she was a natural and how perhaps she ought to think about becoming a show jumper, etc. and so forth, in immense detail.

As I may have said before, Sam has this really loud voice. There just wasn't any way I could compete. So in the end I stopped trying.

First of all, we had to buy Anna her shoes. They were only ordinary shoes for school, but the woman who served us kept oohing and aahing about what beautiful feet she had. Beautiful feet! I ask you!

'So slender . . . such lovely arches! And look at that . . . three toes all the same length. They'd come in handy if you were doing ballet.'

'Oh, but she is,' gurgled Mum.

'Well! There you go,' said the woman. 'A dancer's feet . . . you can always tell!'

'Why are three toes useful?' demanded Sam, as we made our way to the dress department.

'Three toes the same length,' said Anna. 'It makes it easier when you go on point.'

I wondered if I had three toes the same length. I'd never thought to look, but I didn't expect that I had. Sam might; not me.

We all tried helping Mum choose her dress.

Even the Radish! He wanted her to buy this incredible glittery thing all covered in sequins. His face fell a mile when Mum said it was about twenty years too young for her, so in the end she said she'd give everything a go – my dress, Sam's dress, Anna's dress, her own dress, and the sequins.

'I'll try yours first,' she promised the Radish.

'It won't suit her,' whispered Anna, urgently, as Mum went into the changing-room.

A few seconds later, Mum reappeared. A vision!

'Ta da, ta da! How's this?'

Mum did a little twirl. The Radish squealed and pummelled his cheeks. Sam and me both giggled. Mum, in sequins!

'Snazzy, eh?' said Mum.

She winked, to show us that she wasn't serious, but Anna looked quite shocked.

'It doesn't suit her at *all*,' she whispered.

My dress didn't suit her, either; I have to admit it. Neither did Sam's. I'd chosen bright red: Sam had chosen black. Mum herself had chosen powder blue.

'Oh, dear!' she said, ruefully. 'It makes me look like a sack of potatoes. You're so lucky, Anna! You're so tiny. You could wear anything!'

I sneaked a glance at myself in one of the full-length mirrors. I was quite tiny, after all my healthy living. I could wear anything! But I'd given up expecting Mum to notice.

In the end she bought the dress that Anna had picked. I'd thought it was dead boring before she tried it on, but it did actually look quite smart.

'What it is to have dress sense!' sighed Mum. 'I suppose it's all part and parcel of being a dancer. I wish you could come with me every time, Anna!'

She talked about it all the way home in the car. She even told Dad about it, when we sat down to tea.

'Anna's found me *such* a beautiful dress! It makes me look positively sylph-like!'

'That'll be the day!' chuckled Dad.

'Oh, I promise you! You won't recognise the fat lady,' said Mum.

Mum is certainly on the plump side; but so what? Being thin isn't everything. I didn't think she ought to put herself down like that. Dad obviously felt the same. He said, 'I happen to like my fat lady just the way she is.' And he leaned across the table and gave Mum a big smacker of a kiss.

Good old Dad!

He wanted to know what else we'd done that day. Eagerly, I opened my mouth.

'I've b—'

'I went over my first jump!' bellowed Sam.

'Did you now?' said Dad.

'Yes, I did! And I stayed on. Not many people do, over their first jump.'

And then we heard all over again how Sam was a natural.

'Next week I'm going to ride Jet. He's part-Arab. He's really fast!'

'Well, just be careful,' said Dad. 'We don't want any broken bones.'

'Dad,' I said, 'I've been ch—'

'So funny!' chortled Mum, clattering a dish of spaghetti on to the table. 'The woman in the shoe shop guessed at once that Anna was a dancer, didn't she, Anna?'

'No, she didn't,' I said. 'She said *if* she was a dancer. If she was *doing* dancing.'

'Well, but she wasn't surprised!'

'Anyway,' I said, 'I've been ch—'

'Apparently she's got three toes all the same length,' said Mum.

'So've I!' cried Sam. 'Look!'

And she peeled off her sock and plonked one of her great hobnailed feet on the table. And it was true . . . she really did have three toes the same length.

I didn't. I'd looked.

I gave up after that. I didn't bother trying to tell Dad about the competition. He probably wouldn't have been interested, anyway.

7

In November, Anna had to travel up to London for her Young Dancer competition. It was on a Saturday, and Mum insisted on going with her. I couldn't think why. Two other girls from her ballet school were going, so it wasn't like she'd be on her own.

'You're getting to be one of those horrible ballet mothers,' I told Mum. 'Those ones you read about who scratch people's eyes out if their little darlings don't win.'

Mum laughed. 'Oh, Abi,' she said, 'don't be so daft! This is a big day for Anna. I wouldn't let you or Sam go off on your own.'

I said, 'She wouldn't *be* on her own.'

But Mum stood firm. 'The other mums are going to be there. It wouldn't be fair on Anna if she was the only person without anyone.'

I grumbled to Sam about it.

'She's going to be away *all day*.'

Sam just shrugged. It didn't seem to bother her.

'It's not fair!' I said. 'She never does things with you and me.'

'She would,' said Sam, 'if we were going somewhere.'

'Not if Anna was, as well! She'd say we could manage on our own. She'd go with Anna.'

'So what?' said Sam.

'So it's not fair!'

'It is, 'cos she's younger than us. You know what Mum was like when we were her age. Anyway, you were the one who said that if a person was a prodigy the family had to revolve round them!'

It's extremely irritating when people cast your own words up at you.

'Anna's not a prodigy!' I retorted.

'She might be,' said Sam. 'She's really good.'

'Only at ballet.'

'So she's a *ballet* prodigy! Nothing wrong with ballet,' said Sam.

I rushed in, triumphantly.

'That's not what you said before! You said it was *girly*.'

'That was when I didn't know anything about it.'

I looked at Sam with narrowed eyes. Something had happened, since that day in the garden. Sam had actually seen Anna dancing – she had seen her twisting and turning, and leaping and spinning, just like John Travolta in the film – and it had really impressed her. I'd never thought that Sam, of all people, would be impressed!

'That wasn't ballet,' I said, 'what she did in the garden.'

'I know it wasn't,' said Sam.

'That was *disco*.'

'I know it was disco!'

'Anyone can do disco.'

'No, they can't,' said Sam. 'You can't, for a

start, 'cos you're not a dancer!'

I felt my cheeks begin to sizzle.

'Anna can,' said Sam. 'She was brilliant!'

Sam set off across the garden, twisting and turning, leaping and spinning, showing me just how brilliant Anna had been. I started to say, 'You can do it just as well as her,' but then I had a fit of the real meanies and said, 'You're nowhere near as good as she is!'

It wasn't even true. I guess I just wanted to be hurtful.

' 'Course I'm not as good as she is,' scoffed Sam, doing this incredible thing where she fell to her knees and shot back up again all in one snaky kind of movement. 'She's been doing it since she was five years old!'

'*Ballet*,' I said.

'Yeah, but it makes you supple,' said Sam. And she threw herself over backwards and began walking about, upside down, on all fours.

'I still don't see why Mum has to give up her Saturday,' I whined.

I was in a real mood about it. I'd been in a mood ever since half-term. It didn't help that Sam seemed to have crossed over to the other side. I'd have felt a whole lot better if we could have had a good old moan together. It was what we usually did. But she wouldn't get worked up, no matter how hard I tried. She'd become a groupie, just like Mum! So in the end I had a go at Anna, instead.

'You know this competition thing . . . do you have to have Mum go with you?'

'I don't *have* to,' said Anna.

'Do you actually want her to?'

'Well . . . I think she might quite enjoy it,' said Anna. 'She's really interested.'

She wasn't interested in me and my art competition. She'd never once asked me how my picture of Felix was coming along.

Saturday morning, soon as breakfast was over, I went upstairs and lugged my easel and my paints down to the sitting-room, where there's a lot of natural light that comes through the French windows.

'I'm putting newspaper on the floor,' I announced, loudly, for Mum's benefit.

'Newspaper on the – oh, yes!' said Mum. 'Good girl!'

'I'm going to get on with my painting for the art competition.'

'That's a good idea,' said Mum. 'That'll keep you busy.'

'I shall probably spend all day at it.'

'All day!' Mum was flying about, as usual, trying to find her bag and her glasses and her car keys, ready to drive Anna up to town. 'When does it have to be in by?'

'Next week.'

'My goodness! That doesn't give you much time. Do you think you'll be able to manage it?'

'It's nearly finished,' I said. Mum would have known, if only she'd taken a bit more interest. But she'd never asked, so I hadn't told her. 'I decided to paint Felix but make him a Persian Blue. Look!'

I stood back from the easel. Mum paused for about a nanosecond.

'Oh, yes! That's lovely. It looks just like Felix.'

'Do you really think so?'

'Yes, I do!' Mum stuffed her hand down the side of the sofa. '*There* are my glasses! What on earth are they doing there?'

'Do you like the way I've made him be different sorts of blue according to how the light shines? See, he's in shadow here, so it's like a *deep* blue. But this bit, where he's in the sunshine—'

'Oh, sweetheart, you do have the knack of choosing the wrong moment!' said Mum. She bent, and gave me a quick kiss. 'I must dash, or we'll be late! Show me your picture this evening, I'll be able to concentrate on it then.'

Mum flew across to the door.

'Are you going to come and wish Anna good luck?'

I would have liked to be churlish and say no. I was feeling churlish. I was feeling really mean. But sometimes you have to make a bit of an effort, so I trailed out to the hall and said, 'Hope you do well.'

Sam, and Dad, and the Radish all went kissy-kissy. Mum and Dad had actually sent her a good luck card with a black cat on it. Her dad had sent her a telegram, all the way from Hong Kong. Other people had sent her cards, as well. Her ballet teacher, and people from her ballet school.

'We ought to have sent one!' cried Sam, as the car pulled away. 'You could have drawn one for her! You're good at doing cats.'

'I've been busy with my competition entry,' I said.

I spent all day working on my painting. The Radish came to look at it and said, 'It'th a cat like Felikth!'

Dear little Radish! He's so sweet at times. He told Dad about it over lunch – 'Abi'th done a cat jutht like Felikth!' – so Dad and Sam both came to have a look as well.

'I told you you were good at cats!' said Sam.

'You'll probably win first prize.'

'It's for a competition, is it?' said Dad. I still hadn't told him. 'Well, I reckon that's ace! When will you know if you've won?'

'Dunno,' I said, trying to make out it wasn't important.

'Anna has to wait till next month,' said Sam. 'I think that's awful, keeping her in suspense all that time!'

'Yes, there's a lot depending on it,' said Dad. 'It would make life much easier if she could get a scholarship. Mind you—' he chuckled – 'even if she doesn't, she'll still end up as a dancer! She may look like the fairy off the top of the Christmas tree, but she's got a will of steel, that one. She'll get there no matter what.'

And then he glanced again at my painting and said, 'It's a good likeness. Have you shown it to Felix?'

'No,' I said. 'He'd scratch it.' And I picked up my easel, and my paints, and the painting, and trundled them back upstairs to my bedroom.

It was teatime when Mum and Anna got back. Mum had said not to bother getting a meal ready, she'd bring something in – 'for a treat. As it's a special occasion!'

'I thought we'd go Chinese,' she said, spreading dishes on the kitchen table. 'Sit down, all of you, and tuck in!'

'Not till we've heard how things went,' said Dad. 'We've been on tenterhooks all day! What do you reckon?'

Anna said she thought that she had done 'Quite well.' She was always confident, in a quiet and rather maddening sort of way, but she never actually boasted. It was Mum who boasted!

'She didn't just do quite well, she did brilliantly!'

How would Mum know, I wondered? Mum couldn't tell an *arabesque* from a *fouetté*; and anyway, they surely wouldn't have let her in while Anna was dancing?

'I overheard one of the other girls telling her mother.' Mum nodded, all beaming and excited.

'She was in tears, poor little soul! She kept saying how she'd messed everything up and if anyone was going to get the scholarship it would be Anna.'

'That was Lucy Jessop,' said Anna. 'She's always like that. It doesn't mean anything. She didn't really mess up.'

'Well, she seemed to think you were streets ahead of her.'

'We all say that sort of thing,' said Anna. 'Like there was this girl in front of me at the barre who just had this most incredible turn-out!' She made her eyes go wide, to show us how incredible it was. 'And then there was this other girl, in *adage*, she was just so classy! She had this really beautiful line.'

'I'm sure you have a beautiful line,' said Mum.

'Not like this girl.' Anna swivelled her big dark eyes in Mum's direction. 'When she did an arabesque, it was like . . . like floating!'

And she pushed back her chair and did this arabesque to demonstrate.

'What's wrong with that?' Mum wanted to know.

'There's nothing *wrong* with it,' said Anna. She said it very earnestly. 'It's just not floating.'

'Looks like floating to me,' said Dad.

What did Dad know about it? He knew even less than Mum!

I leaned forward and helped myself greedily to every dish on the table. The others could wait if they liked, but I was hungry! I'd given up trying to be like Anna; she wasn't my role model any more. I was back to eating cheese-and-onion crisps. Such a relief! Life had been really empty without my cheese-and-onion crisps. Of course, I would soon be back to being roly poly, as well, but who cared? Not me! Nobody had noticed when I was thin, so what was the point? I firmly believe that we all have our own shapes, and if mine is roly poly, *so what?*

'You don't mind, do you?' I whispered to Jack, upstairs in my horrible broom cupboard later that evening.

Jack licked my face and assured me that he didn't. He loved me whatever shape I was! It is one of the joys of dogs: they never sit in judgement on you.

We had spent simply hours, after dinner, talking about Anna and how she'd done in the competition. I'd never heard her be so animated before. She kept remembering something else to tell us about. How for instance she had mistimed one of her jumps and landed really badly and one of the examiners had immediately started making notes on a sheet of paper.

'She was marking me down, I know she was!'

'Nonsense!' said Mum. 'No one is perfect. They wouldn't expect it.'

Then she told us how one girl had turned the wrong way and bumped into her, and thrown her off balance.

'It was awful! I nearly died!'

'Hardly your fault,' said Mum. 'They won't hold that against you.'

Another girl had shown up wearing a white leotard, gasp horror!

'We were all supposed to be wearing *black*.'

Mum sucked in her breath. 'How dreadful! What happened?'

'They let her continue,' said Anna, 'but they weren't very pleased.'

'I should think not! She won't be getting any scholarship.'

'Nor will I,' sighed Anna. 'I made *so* many mistakes. I just realised something!'

'What, what?' said Mum.

'I did the wrong steps!' Anna clapped a hand to her mouth. 'I wondered why it didn't work! I did *this*—' she twizzled across the room in a series of tiny little sideways shuffles – 'instead of this!' And she twizzled back again, doing what looked to me to be exactly the same thing.

It obviously looked the same to Mum, as well.

'Oh, I'm sure they won't have noticed!' she said, cheerfully. 'Don't go losing any sleep over it!'

Mum never once asked me about my painting of Felix. I'd kind of hoped the Radish might have mentioned it.

'Abi'th painted *Felikth*!'

But even the Radish seemed to have forgotten all about it.

Up in my loathsome broom cupboard, I sat on the bed, cuddling Jack and staring at my painting, trying to decide if it was really any good or if it was just chocolate-boxy.

Chocolate-boxy was what Mr Martin called pictures that were just sweet and pretty without any real depth. Like if you were to paint a dear little fluffy kitten that made people go 'Ooh' and 'Aah' but didn't have anything properly *cat*-like about it. A chocolate-box kitten that never pounced or stalked or leapt or sprang. Just sat on a cushion with a box in its hair.

Could I imagine my Persian Blue Felix pouncing and leaping? I thought that I could; but it was so difficult to be sure! I wouldn't really

know until I showed it to Mr Martin. If his face
lit up – hurray! If it didn't–

'Abi?'

There was a knock on the door, and Mum's
head appeared.

'Can I come in? Dad was telling me about your
picture . . . oh! There it is. Let me have a proper
look at it, I didn't have time this morning.'

Mum studied it, her head to one side.

'Now that,' she said, 'is what I call really
beautiful!'

'It's all right,' I said.

'No, it's lovely! What a clever girl you are!'

I cringed. I felt sure she was only saying it
because she'd forgotten and she felt guilty.

'Do you think it looks like Felix?' I said.

'Of course it does! I recognised him
immediately.'

'But do you think it looks like a *real* Felix or
just a chocolate-box Felix?'

Needless to say, Mum didn't know what I was
talking about. I had to explain.

'Does it look as if he could climb trees and stalk birds?'

'Oh, definitely!' said Mum. 'He has a very wicked glint in his eye!' And then she sat down on the bed and put her arm round me and said, 'Abi, I know you've been feeling neglected just lately. I'm sorry, pet! I haven't meant to ignore you. It's just that this competition is so important for Anna! Her whole future's at stake. And what with her nan dying, and her dad being in Hong Kong – well! She's needed a lot of support. You do understand, don't you?'

I nodded, but out of the corner of my eye I'd caught sight of the stupid pink ballet shoes that I'd bought. They were sticking out from under the chest. I did hope Mum couldn't see them! I wished now that I'd never wasted my money on them. I couldn't ever be like Anna, however hard I tried! I couldn't imagine, now, why I'd wanted to be. I was *me*. And I was going to art school. And now I'd have to start saving up all over again for my oil paints!

Mum stood up. I quickly kicked the shoes out of sight. Maybe one day, in a few months' time, I'd cut the ribbons off and use them as ordinary slippers.

'I just wanted you to know,' said Mum, 'that I hadn't forgotten about you. All right?'

I nodded again.

'From now on, things will be back to normal. That's a promise!'

8

Well! All I can say is that Mum's idea of normal isn't the same as mine.

My idea of normal is Mum being there when me and Sam get back from school, and staying there while we have our tea. It's Mum wanting to know what's new in our lives. Wanting to know what marks we got for our homework and what we've had for school dinner. Not racing to and fro collecting people from ballet lessons and fussing and flapping about when they were going to hear whether they'd won a scholarship.

'I do wonder when they'll let her know?'

'I wonder when they'll let *me* know?' I said.

'Now, don't go getting your hopes up too high,' warned Mum. 'They must have had dozens of entries.'

There must have been dozens of people trying for scholarships, but Mum didn't tell Anna not to get her hopes up too high. It was like they didn't really take me seriously. In spite of saying how lovely my painting was, and how it looked just like Felix, they didn't expect me to actually win anything.

But when I gave the painting to Mr Martin, to be put in for the competition, his face lit up, just as I'd hoped it would. 'Abi,' he said, 'this is the best thing you've ever done!' So I knew that *he* thought I stood a chance.

I said, 'It's not chocolate-boxy, is it?'

I was still anxious about that; I still hadn't been able to decide. I worried that I might have made it too pretty. Felix is *not* pretty; he is extremely beautiful and handsome, and very lithe and sleek. If only he were stripy, instead of white, you could imagine him slinking through the jungle after his prey.

'Just because he's fluffy,' I said, earnestly, 'it doesn't mean he's not a real cat!'

Mr Martin told me to relax.

'This cat is red in tooth and claw! Look at the

expression on his face . . . look at the way he's crouched . . . any minute now he's going to spring!'

Nobody else had noticed that; only Mr Martin! It was because he was a real art person.

I spent the rest of the day walking on air! I kept wanting to rush off to the art studio and take another look at my painting, so that I could study the way Felix was crouched and admire the expression on his face. Once I would have gone running home to share my excitement with Mum, but now I hugged it to myself. I didn't think Mum would properly appreciate the importance of what Mr Martin had said.

'Any minute now he's going to spring!'

She'd say, 'Oh, well, that's nice then. He obviously likes it.'

She wouldn't understand. You had to be a real art person to understand.

As well as going in for her competition, Anna was also dancing in her end-of-term show. She was going to be a pierrot, wearing a white satiny jumpsuit with bright red pom poms all the way down and a little white hat, also with a pom pom. *Mum* was making the costume. As if she didn't have enough to do!

'I never knew you could sew,' I said, accusingly.

'Oh, yes!' said Mum. 'When I first got married I used to make all my own clothes. I was a dab hand with a needle!'

'You've never made me anything,' I said.

'I offered,' said Mum. 'When your school had a book week, do you remember? You all got dressed up. I offered to make you a Red Riding Hood outfit, but you said you wouldn't wear it?'

I'd forgotten about that. I'd thought I'd look silly dressed up as Red Riding Hood so I'd gone in a T-shirt and jeans and called myself George from *Five on a Treasure Island*.

'You had your chance,' said Mum. 'Pass me a pom pom!'

Sam was eager to know if we could all go and watch.

'Of course we'll go and watch!' said Mum. 'I

wouldn't miss it for the world!'

I was really amazed at Sam. Wanting to go and watch Anna dance around in red pom poms! Once she'd have said it was dead naff, not to mention *girly*. Now she kept asking Anna to teach her the steps, and before we knew it there were two of them twirling and leaping and pom-pom-pomming about the place.

'You could be a dancer!' cried Anna.

'Nah,' said Sam. 'Gonna teach PE!'

But she blushed – almost the first time I had *ever* seen Sam blush – so I knew that secretly she was flattered.

One day Mum came back from fetching Anna from her ballet class with this huge big beam on her face.

'Guess what?' she said.

'What?' Me and Sam sprang round from the television.

'Tell them, Anna!'

'I've got the scholarship.'

She didn't shout it out as Sam or me would

have done; just announced it in this very matter-of-fact voice like it wasn't anything so terribly special. She wasn't at all a demonstrative kind of person, except for when she was dancing, but her eyes were shining and you could tell that there was a lot of quiet satisfaction going on underneath.

'Isn't that wonderful news?' said Mum.

'*Wow!*' Sam gave this blood-curdling shriek and hurled herself across the room. She flung her arms round Anna's neck. 'That is fan*tastic!*'

'Miss Heriot's delighted,' said Mum. 'And her dad's going to be absolutely thrilled! Let's go and send him an e-mail!'

Mum and Sam and Anna went charging off to the front room, which is Mum's office where the computer is kept. The Radish scuttled after them. I was left on my own.

I thought, 'I'm really pleased she's got her scholarship.'

Somehow, it didn't quite ring true. I tried it again.

'I'm really pleased, I really am!'

It still didn't ring true. But I was pleased! It would have been mean not to be. There wasn't any reason not to be. I *was* pleased! I was!

But I still didn't feel that I was. It was just something I was saying, 'cos I knew that was how I ought to feel.

I sat in front of the television, trying to pretend that I was watching the programme. But I couldn't even do that! It was like I had this pit of evil green slime bubbling away inside me, all seething and heaving and threatening to spew out. Ugh! Disgusting!

I thought that when the others came back I would force myself to say 'Congratulations,' just to show how civilised I was. But they came bursting through the door, Sam and Anna with their arms linked, doing Anna's pierrot dance, with the Radish giggling and kicking his legs in the air, and Mum laughing along behind, and it made me feel really left out.

I snatched up Jack and cuddled him, fiercely,

but even Jack didn't want to be with me. He wanted to jump down and be part of the fun! Even Daisy grinned and clapped her paws.

Only me and Felix didn't join in. Felix was perched on top of the television, watching the proceedings with a most disagreeable expression on his face. I knew how he felt! I wished I could go and perch on the television with him.

When Dad came in, Sam shouted, 'Anna's got her scholarship!'

Dad was just as excited as everyone else.

'That's wonderful news,' he said. 'All set for stardom, now, eh?'

'We've e-mailed her dad,' giggled Mum. 'In a few years' time, girls, we'll be telling everyone how we knew Anna Margolis before she became famous!'

'Imagine if you were called something awful,' said Sam. 'Anna *Pea*body, Anna *Side*bottom . . . imagine having a ballet dancer called Sidebottom!'

'She's lucky,' said Mum. 'She's got a lovely

name. Did they call you Anna after Anna Pavlova, do you think?'

'Who's Anna Pabloba?' I said.

'Pav-*lo*-va,' said Sam.

'So who is she?'

'*Was*,' said Sam. 'She was a famous ballerina.'

I wondered how Sam knew. The only pavlova I'd heard of was the raspberry sort, with cream and meringue.

'She danced the Dying Swan,' said Anna; and she jumped up from the table and did this fluttering thing with her arms, beating like swan's wings, then very slowly sank down with one leg tucked under her, the other stretched straight out in front, and still fluttering let her head fall forward on to her knee, with her arms curved over.

We all stopped eating, to watch. Even me. I didn't want to, but I couldn't not.

Showing off, I thought. But it wasn't. Anna never showed off.

'Me, me!' cried Sam. 'Let me!'

She pushed back her chair and began doing what Anna had done. She fluttered her arms and sank down on to one leg and let her head fall forward on to her knee. But Sam didn't really look like a dying swan. She was too energetic.

'Swan having convulsions,' said Dad.

Sam stuck her tongue out.

'You stick to your gymnastics,' said Dad. 'Anna's the ballerina, you can be the Olympic gold medallist. How's that?'

I felt like saying, 'What about me?' But of course I didn't. That's the sort of thing you say when you're six years old. By the time you get to be eleven, you have a bit more pride.

'Come Saturday, we'll have a celebration,' burbled Mum. 'We'll get a bottle of champagne!'

Champagne??? Even Sam's mouth gaped open. We'd never ever had champange!

Silly old Raspberry Pavlova, I muttered, as I got ready for bed later that evening. Raspberry Pavlova! I wished I could share the joke with Sam. Usually when we thought of funny names for people, like for instance the Radish, we got together and giggled over them. But I just had this feeling Sam wouldn't find Raspberry Pavlova amusing. She'd become a real groupie!

It was on Tuesday when Anna heard about her scholarship. Her dad rang up all the way from Hong Kong to congratulate her.

'He's coming back in time for the end-of-term show,' she told us.

I suppose she was excited. Well, I think she must have been 'cos she went spinning off round the room. If I'd done that, or even Sam, we'd probably have smashed a few vases or overturned a few chairs, but Anna never broke things or bumped into things. She was Little Miss Perfect!

Then on Thursday, Mr Martin told me I'd won my section in the art competition. I was the only one to have won anything! From our school, I mean. (Though one girl got Highly Commended.) The prize-giving was to be held the following Wednesday in the Town Hall, during the lunch hour.

'Be prepared to have your photo taken,' said Mr Martin. 'The local paper's going to be there. You'll be a celebrity!'

There was one bit of me that was dying to rush home and tell Mum – 'I've won! I'm going to be famous!' But there was another bit, a little stubborn bit, that wouldn't let me. The little stubborn bit kept saying, 'Don't tell *anyone*. Let them find out for themselves!'

I suppose it was silly, really; but it was the way that I felt.

Then next morning, in assembly, they went and announced it. In front of the whole school!

'Abigail Foster has won the Under-Thirteen section of the Borough Schools Art Competition, and Joella Metcalfe has been Highly Commended.'

Everyone clapped, and me and Joella had to go up on stage and have our hands shaken. It was rather embarrassing, with the whole school watching, especially as I went and tripped over my feet on the way up the steps.

Afterwards, Sam wanted to know all about it.

'When d'you get your prize?'

'Next week.'

'What is it? What d'you get?'

'Oh, nothing very much,' I said. 'Only £50 worth of oil paints.'

'*Only?*' said Sam.

'Well. You know!' I shrugged. 'It's not like a *scholarship*.'

Sam looked at me, eyes narrowed.

'Have you got a cob on?'

She's always coming out with these weird expressions. Very often I haven't the faintest idea what she's talking about.

'Are you in a *mood*?'

'No,' I said. 'Why should I be?'

'Can't imagine,' said Sam. 'Considering you've just won £50 worth of oil paints! I thought it was what you wanted?'

I humped a shoulder.

'It's what you *said* you wanted! You said you were saving up to buy some. What's the matter with you? Aren't you happy?'

'Yes,' I said, 'but you're not to tell Mum. Or Dad. Or anyone!'

Sam stared at me.

'Why not?'

' 'Cos I don't want you to!'

'Why don't you want me to?'

' 'Cos they wouldn't be interested.'

' 'Course they'd be interested!'

'I don't care. You're not to tell them!'

I made Sam promise. Mum could wait till she saw my photo in the local paper. Or till she bumped into someone in Tesco and they'd say, 'I saw your daughter's picture,' and Mum, totally bewildered, would say, 'Which daughter?' and they'd say, 'The one who won the art competition!' And it would be the first that Mum knew about it! She'd ask me why I hadn't told her, and I'd say, 'I didn't think you'd be interested. It's not like winning a scholarship.' And Mum would be covered in confusion.

Well, that's how I pictured it. But it didn't quite work out that way.

I knew Mum was preparing for Anna's celebration 'cos Saturday afternoon she told me and Sam to get out from under her feet, and actually gave us some money and sent us into town to mooch round the shopping centre. Anna came with us. We mooched until five o'clock, when the pangs of hunger drove us home.

'Hope she's ready for us,' said Sam. 'My gut is hanging out!'

Another of her weird expressions. I don't know *where* she gets them from.

Mum wouldn't let us into the kitchen. She said, 'Off you go upstairs and get changed! You can't sit down to a celebration dressed like that. Best clothes, please! Pretend you're going to a restaurant.'

I went grumbling up to my bedroom with Jack. I wasn't going to get all dressed up just for silly old Raspberry Pavlova!

'I hate her,' I said to Jack. 'I hate all of them! I hate her and I hate Sam and I hate Mum and I hate Dad!'

Then I burst into tears, which is something I almost never do. Hate, hate, *hate*! I went, thumping at my pillow. Ever since Anna had come to us, she had been Little Miss Perfect. The centre of attention. Hogging all the limelight. And she'd never been grateful! Never, not once!

At six o'clock, Mum came out into the hall and beat with a wooden spoon on a tin tray.

'Ladies and gentlemen . . . dinner is served!'

I almost felt like saying I wasn't hungry. But I was! I was starving! I picked myself off the bed and scrubbed at my eyes and went out on to the landing just as Sam came galloping out of her bedroom.

'You haven't changed!' she said.

No, I hadn't. And I jolly well wasn't going to!

'You'll catch it,' said Sam.

Huh! What did I care?

Slowly I followed Sam and Little Miss Perfect downstairs.

'Grub!' cried Sam, doing a grand *jeté* off the last step.

Anna giggled, and jumped after her. Showing off, I thought sourly.

Mum was standing at the kitchen door.

'Enter!' she said.

I couldn't believe it! She'd hung coloured streamers all across the kitchen and put the special Christmas table cloth on the kitchen table and got the silver candlesticks out that had belonged to Auntie Marge. All this, just for silly old Raspberry Pavlova!

'Take your seats,' said Mum.

We all sat down. My eyes goggled. There were little flute-shaped glasses with wiggly stems, and posh pink napkins, all crisp and starched, folded to look like water lilies. And in the middle of the table were two cakes. One was shaped like a ballet shoe, with pink satin ribbons – real ones – and a little card propped inside. On the card was written, 'Well done, Anna!' The other one . . .

The other one was shaped like a cat. It had whiskers made out of plastic bristles, and round its neck it wore a jewelled collar. Tied to the collar was another little card. This one said, 'Well done, Abi!'

I felt my cheeks go bright pink. I sprang round, accusingly, on Sam.

'You told them!'

' 'Course I did,' said Sam.

'Of course she did,' said Mum.

'You broke your promise!'

'So what?' said Sam.

So now it was my celebration as well as Anna's. And I couldn't pretend not to be pleased!

But the biggest surprise of all was Anna! She suddenly jumped up and grabbed my hands and pulled me to my feet, and before I knew it we were dancing all round the kitchen together!

'Abi'th danthing!' squeaked the Radish; and

he pummelled at his cheeks and made this little crowing noise.

Anna didn't say to me, like she'd said to Sam, that I could be a dancer. What she said was, 'Isn't it fun? We've both of us won!' Like she was really happy that it was both of us and not just her.

'Break open the champagne!' cried Dad. 'Let's have a toast!'

Mum and Dad, and Sam and the Radish, all raised their glasses.

'Here's to our little ballerina,' said Dad, 'and our budding artist . . . we're extremely proud of you both!'

What about Sam? I wondered, anxiously.

But Sam didn't seem in the least jealous or put out. She really is the best sister in the whole wide world!

The following week I went to collect my prize and have my photo taken, and that Friday there were pictures of both me *and* Anna in the local paper. Mum said, 'I can't stop boasting about the pair of you!'

After that, we had Anna's end-of-term show to look forward to, and I really *was* looking forward to it. Now that I no longer had that pit of horrible green slime inside me!

Anna's dad was coming to the show, and then he was going to take her off with him, which meant that I would be able to have my bedroom back, and I must admit I was quite looking forward to that, as well. It is very limiting, living in a broom cupboard.

The day of the show was a Saturday. The plan was that Anna's dad would fly back from Hong Kong that same day. He would arrive in London early in the afternoon and come straight over. That way, he could spend an hour or so with Anna before she was whisked away to the theatre to get changed for the performance. (One of the other girls, with her mum, was going to pick her up. The rest of us, including Anna's dad, were going to follow later.)

Well. Two o'clock arrived and we still hadn't had a phone call to say that the plane had landed.

'I expect there's been a bit of a delay,' said Dad. 'Not unusual.'

But then it got to be three o'clock and we still hadn't heard, and that was worrying, so Dad rang the airport and guess what? The plane wasn't just a *bit* delayed, it was *hugely* delayed. It wasn't expected to land until six o'clock!

'Well, at least we know he's on his way,' said Mum, trying to be cheerful.

At quarter past six the phone still hadn't rung and the other girl had arrived in the car with her mum to take Anna to the theatre. Mum gave Anna a hug and said, 'Don't worry, pet! He'll make it.' But I didn't really see how he could. I don't think Mum did, either.

Anna didn't say anything; she just gave Mum this soulful look out of her big dark eyes as she climbed into the back of the car.

'Poor little love,' said Mum. 'This is her big day, and her dad's not here to see it!'

I still wasn't sure how much Anna really cared. If that had been my dad, stuck up there in an aeroplane, I'd have been chewing my fingernails down to stumps.

I wasn't really sure how much Anna cared about anything, except her dancing.

At seven o'clock we still hadn't had a phone call and Dad said we'd have to be setting off.

'We can't wait any longer.'

'This is so sad!' said Sam.

'She won't mind,' I said. 'The only thing she thinks about is her dancing.'

But that was where I was wrong. We'd no sooner reached the theatre than this woman came running up to us, all distraught and wringing her hands. It was the woman who'd picked Anna up in her car.

'She won't dance!' she cried. 'She's in tears! She says she wants her dad! She won't even listen to Miss Heriot!'

I suppose it's not what's called *professional*, but it did make me warm towards her.

'Where is she?' said Mum. 'Let me go and talk to her.'

Mum told us afterwards that if the miracle hadn't occurred – if Anna's dad hadn't come racing through the doors at almost literally the last minute – Anna wouldn't have gone on. It just shows that you don't always know what people are really like, deep down.

We all heaved a huge sigh of relief as the curtain went up, and there was Anna, in her pierrot costume, along with all the others. You would never have guessed that only a few minutes earlier she'd been sitting in the dressing-room crying her eyes out because she wanted her dad.

At the end of her solo, we all clapped like anything. Not just us! The whole theatre.

'She's really good, isn't she?' whispered Mum. And then quickly she squeezed my hand and added, 'And so are you!'

Mum didn't have to say that. Anna was special, and I think we all knew it.

'But it will be nice,' said Sam, as we walked the dogs in the park next morning, 'just being me and you again. Not that Anna's been any *bother*. I mean, she didn't push herself forward or get in the way, or anything. But you couldn't ever really get close to her. Remember when we started calling ourselves the superglue kids?'

'Mm!' I nodded.

'You couldn't ever be superglue kids with Anna. Know what I'm saying?'

'Yes; I think so.'

'She's nice, but . . . she's not like you and me.'

'Maybe that's because we're just ordinary people,' I said.

'What, you mean like she's a prodigy?'

'Well . . . she's different.'

We walked for a while in silence.

'Would you like to be different?' said Sam.

I linked my arm through Sam's.

'I'd rather be superglue kids!' I said.